T0001276

GREEK MYTHS

Gods and Goddesses

More classic literature available
from Macmillan Collector's Library

Greek Myths: Heroes and Heroines
edited by Jean Menzies

The Odyssey by Homer

The Iliad by Homer

The Aeneid by Virgil

GREEK MYTHS

Gods and Goddesses

Edited and introduced by
JEAN MENZIES

MACMILLAN COLLECTOR'S LIBRARY

This collection first published 2023 by Macmillan Collector's Library
an imprint of Pan Macmillan
The Smithson, 6 Briset Street, London ECIM 5NR
EU representative: Macmillan Publishers Ireland Ltd, 1st Floor,
The Liffey Trust Centre, 117–126 Sheriff Street Upper,
Dublin 1, D01 YC43
Associated companies throughout the world
www.panmacmillan.com

ISBN 978-1-5290-9334-6

Selection and introductions © Jean Menzies 2023

All rights reserved. No part of this publication may be reproduced,
stored in a retrieval system, or transmitted, in any form, or by any means
(electronic, mechanical, photocopying, recording or otherwise)
without the prior written permission of the publisher.

1 3 5 7 9 8 6 4 2

A CIP catalogue record for this book is available from the British Library.

Casing design and endpaper pattern by Andrew Davidson
Typeset by Jouve (UK), Milton Keynes
Printed and bound in China by Imago

This book is sold subject to the condition that it shall not, by way of
trade or otherwise, be lent, hired out, or otherwise circulated without
the publisher's prior consent in any form of binding or cover other than
that in which it is published and without a similar condition including
this condition being imposed on the subsequent purchaser.

MIX
Paper | Supporting
responsible forestry
FSC® C116313

Visit **www.panmacmillan.com** to read more
about all our books and to buy them.

Contents

Introduction

JEAN MENZIES

Mythology, something so inextricably tied to antiquity in our imaginations, is in fact an entirely modern word. While the term finds its origin in combining the ancient Greek words *mythos* and *logos*, mythology as we know it today first reared its head in the fifteenth-century poem *Troy Book* by the monk John Lydgate. *Mythos* in ancient Greek had a multitude of meanings, from word to story, both factual and contentious. Unlike the more modern 'mythology', however, there was nothing inherently fictitious about *mythos* itself. Yet this is what we think of when we think about mythology today: fictional and often fantastical tales of daring deeds, malevolent monsters, and, in this instance, Greek gods and goddesses.

So, what distinguishes a myth as we use the word today from any other fictitious tale? The simplest answer is religion. It is easy to forget when we are watching epic adventure films like *Clash of the Titans* or reading insightful retellings like Natalie Haynes's *A Thousand Ships* that the most powerful players in these stories were the subject of worship for thousands of ancient people and, in fact, remain so for many modern-day neopagans. These were the tales of their gods and goddesses. Deities who they poured libations to at gatherings, who they honoured with elaborate festivals, and who they turned to in times of need.

The ancient Greek gods and goddesses were not all benevolence and generosity, however. Although distinct from humans in their power and immortality, these divine beings were just as susceptible to the range of whims and emotions that we are all too familiar with. They experienced jealousy and anger, malice and spite, and they were no strangers to taking out the worst of these moods on the mortal men and women they reigned over. Not only is this reflected in their stories but the way in which they were worshipped; the ire of the ancient Greek gods and goddesses was not something to incur lightly.

It is fascinating, therefore, to think that the stories of these deities, who were both respected and feared by their followers, have retained so much significance even outside of their original religious context. From the fifth-century-BCE theatres of Athens to the twenty-first-century cinema screens of Britain, stories concerning the ancient Greek gods and goddesses have captured the imaginations of countless audiences. Yet, while it might seem to the casual consumer that myth has had a recent resurgence, this could not be further from the truth. The myths concerning the ancient Greek gods and goddesses did not lie in slumber for thousands of years waiting to be reread and retold by modern readers and writers. Nor did they exist solely within circles of continuous believers. The power of Greek myths to entertain and to educate has instead carried on uninterrupted for millennia.

This collection specifically brings together a wide selection of Greek myths as retold by writers of the Victorian and Edwardian periods. While several of the authors, including the German Carl Witt and American Emilie Kip Baker, were not residents of Britain where Victoria or Edward reigned, there is an undeniable influence of the times in all their writing. The Victorian era in particular is often remembered for its emphasis on morality and evangelism, with many authors demonstrating their strong ties to Christianity in their writing. Fascinatingly enough, even within these stories of ancient pagan gods and goddesses their contemporary religious themes abound.

In selecting stories for this collection, I tried to choose those, which to my own knowledge as an ancient historian, were most in keeping with at least one or another of the original versions (because even the ancients disagreed). Yet even then the influences of Victorian and Edwardian society peek through, and we should not want it any other way. These retellings of the Greek myths are part of a long tradition started by the ancient Greeks themselves, wherein individuals and groups interpret and even reimagine the tales of these mighty deities according to the values their own culture expounds. While Natalie Haynes's modern retelling of the Trojan war offers a twenty-first-century perspective of Greek myth where women are centred, fourth-century-BCE speech writer Hyperides equally offers a version of the same events that resonate with the values of his contemporary Athenians during their war with the Macedonians. Whether or not they were aware of it at the time, therefore, the authors collected here are just as much a part of the history of Greek myth.

With that said, for every myth about the gods and goddesses of Ancient Greece included in this volume, there are at least two more that are not. When you decide who falls in love with who or whether the seas will be treacherous or calm, a lot of stories develop around you. There does not even exist an ancient Greek text which compiles every mythical variant in one place, let alone one single collection from the nineteenth century. When compiling the stories you will read in this volume, therefore, I aimed to both introduce readers to some of the major events of Greek myth involving their gods and goddesses, while also demonstrating the range of themes present in these tales.

Allow James Baldwin and Emilie Kip Baker to introduce you to the way in which the ancients believed the world was formed, before H. A. Guerber and Lilian Stoughton Hyde share tales from the lives of their deities themselves. Witness the ire of the gods and goddesses unfold in the stories of Carl Witt and Thomas Bullfinch, so you can compare these tales with the sometimes equally devastating consequences of inspiring the love of the gods as narrated by Elsie Finnimore Buckley and Jean Lang. Finally, complete your journey with a reminder of the ways in which the gods and goddesses rewarded their followers with the compelling narratives of Josephine Preston Peabody and, together, Ferdinand Schmidt and Karl Friedrich Becker. Once you have read through each of these stories in turn you will have a strong sense of who the ancient Greeks believed their gods and goddesses to be, their strengths and their foibles, and why they have inspired so much fascination throughout time.

GREEK MYTHS

Gods and Goddesses

CREATION

As with any other civilization, the ancient Greeks were fascinated with the world they lived in, how it worked and how it came to be. For answers they turned to the gods, and thus several myths sprang forth to explain the origins of both their deities and themselves. To fully immerse ourselves in the world of Greek myth, therefore, it makes sense to start at the beginning. Included here are three major events in the creation of the world according to Greek myth. Carl Witt tells the story of earth's beginning and the fight for supremacy between the gods. James Baldwin continues our tale with how man was gifted fire by a sympathetic titan and the creation of Pandora, the very first woman. Finally, Emilie Kip Baker recounts the flood sent by the gods to wipe out humanity when they ceased to show respect, only to be born anew thanks to two humble souls.

The Beginning of All Things

~~~~~~~~~~

Long ago, in the beginning of time, there was nothing but a huge dark mass called Chaos. In this Chaos were hidden all things that now exist, the earth and the sky, light and darkness, fire and water, and everything else, but they were not yet severed one from the other, and were so mingled and confused that nothing had a separate form of its own. After the Chaos had lasted for a long time it parted asunder, and the earth was divided from the heaven. The sun and the moon and the stars mounted up above into the sky, but the water and the stones and the trees liked better to remain below with the earth.

There was a god in the sky called Uranus, and on earth there was a goddess called Gaea. They became husband and wife, and had several children, of whom six were ugly and twelve were beautiful. The ugly ones had, each of them, either a hundred arms, or else only one eye. Those who had a hundred arms had also fifty heads, and they were as big as mountains, and very frightful. The

3

others had only one eye apiece, and it was placed in the middle of their foreheads and was as large as a cart wheel. But the beautiful brothers and sisters were formed like men, only they were much larger and grander. Six of them were gods, and were called Titans; there were also six goddesses, who were called Titanides.

The gods lived on the summit of a very high mountain called Mount Olympus, which almost reached the sky, and Uranus was king over them all. He could not bear the sight of his hundred-armed and one-eyed children because they were so hideous, so he thrust them into a dark pit below the earth, called Tartarus, and would not let them come out of it again. But the mother Gaea loved even her ugly children, and was angry with Uranus for banishing them into darkness and misery. And she said to her son Cronus, who was the youngest of the beautiful gods, that if he would promise to fetch up his hundred-armed and one-eyed brothers out of Tartarus, she would help him to dethrone Uranus and himself become king of the gods. Cronus promised that he would do this, and Gaea created the bright cutting steel, and made with it a sharp sickle which she gave to her son, and told him to kill Uranus with it when he was asleep.

Cronus did as she desired him, and thus Uranus lost his kingdom and his life.*

Cronus now ruled over the world in his father's stead, and the other gods had to obey him. He took one of the Titanides called Rhea, to be his wife, and made her the queen. He also fetched up his ugly brothers from Tartarus, but he soon became afraid of them and drove them back into the dark pit. The mother Gaea now saw how little she had gained by her treachery to her husband, and she told Cronus that he should lose his kingly power through one of his children just as Uranus had done. This frightened him so much that whenever Rhea had a child, he took it and swallowed it. He swallowed five of them in this way, and poor Rhea was very sad because she had no children left. Then Gaea told her, next time she had a child, to take a stone and wrap it in swaddling clothes and give it to Cronus to swallow as if it were the baby, but keep the real child in some safe place till it was grown up. Rhea did so, and Cronus swallowed the stone she gave him, thinking it was the little boy that had just been born, but Rhea hid the child in a cave in the island of Crete where a beautiful goat

* In the ancient versions of the myth Cronos castrates his father rather than killing him.

named Amalthea nourished him with her milk. And there were armed men there, who, whenever the baby cried, danced about and clashed their shields and spears together as if they were treading a war-dance for their own amusement, but it was really to prevent Cronus from hearing the crying. The boy was named Zeus, and in a year he was quite grown up, and was the most beautiful and most powerful of all the gods. When Cronus was asleep, Rhea used to go to the cave and talk to him.

At last the time came when Zeus was to wage war against his father, and then Gaea gave her daughter Rhea a bowl containing a sweet medicine for Cronus to drink. Rhea went to her husband and said, 'The mother Gaea is no longer angry with you, and she has sent you this sweet drink.' Cronus took the bowl and drank it up; it tasted very nice, but after he had swallowed it he began to feel very uncomfortable, and presently he was sick. Then out came the stone and the children that he had swallowed, the youngest first, and the eldest last; there were two gods and three goddesses, and they were all quite grown up. The names of the gods were Poseidon and Hades, and the names of the goddesses were Hera, Demeter, and Hestia.

Then the young gods made war against the old ones, and they sent for the hundred-armed and one-eyed monsters out of Tartarus, that they might help them. The One-eyed were very skilful at smith's work, and they were so grateful to Zeus for setting them free that they forged for him valuable weapons, thunder and lightning. The old gods took their stand on Mount Othrys, and the young ones on Mount Olympus, and between them was a wide far-stretching valley where they fought. When there was a battle the whole earth resounded at the tread of the gods. The Hundred-armed always threw a hundred pieces of rock at once, and Zeus hurled thunderbolt after thunderbolt, till the woods were in flames and the rivers boiled. The war lasted for ten years, but at last the young gods triumphed. They thrust their enemies into Tartarus, and set the Hundred-armed and the One-eyed to keep guard over them.

Zeus was now the king of the gods, and he married his sister Hera and made her the queen. He also gave an empire to each of his brothers: all the sea was made subject to Poseidon, and Hades became king of the Lower World, where the dead are. These gods had children, who were also gods, and had each their part in the government of the universe. The good goat Amalthea was already dead, but Zeus honoured her by making one of her horns a wonder, which became famous all over the world. Whoever had it might wish for anything he liked to eat or drink, and immediately it was there; and for this reason it was called the Horn of Plenty, because it produced in abundance everything that could be desired in the way of food.

The mother Gaea had planned the overthrow of Cronus because he had driven back his hundred-armed and one-eyed brothers into Tartarus. But she found herself worse off than ever, for the only result of her revenge was that now her beautiful children were imprisoned instead of the ugly ones. This made her very angry with the young gods, and she could not bear to see them powerful and happy. So she brought into the world some hideous monsters to make war against the young gods. They were called Giants, and had enormous strength and courage. They tore up masses of rock and dashed them up into the air till the vault of heaven rang again, but the gods only laughed at it, for the stones were powerless to hurt them by the time they had reached so great a height, and there was no mountain high enough for the Giants to climb from it to the top of Mount Olympus.

The Giants went on in this way for a long time, but they found that, do what they would, they could not inflict any injury upon the gods, and only got laughed at for their pains, so they resolved to try another plan. They made up their minds to build a ladder by which they might climb up to the abode of the gods, and they set to work to uproot a mountain called Ossa, and roll it on to the top of another mountain called Pelion. But whilst they were doing this, Zeus hurled a mighty thunderbolt against Ossa and made it fall down again, and the gods rushed down to the earth to fight the Giants, shouting their war-cry. The fight lasted for a whole day, for the Giants were very strong, but at last the gods gained the victory, and they crushed each of the Giants beneath a huge mountain, which did not kill him, but prevented his ever getting up again. One of them tried to escape over the Mediterranean Sea, but the goddess Athene, who was the daughter of Zeus, tore off a great three-cornered piece of land and threw it after him. It hit him just as he was in the middle of the sea, and he fell down and was buried beneath it. After some time the land became covered with forests and cities, and it is now called the Island of Sicily. Every now and then the Giants turn on one side beneath their mountains, and then people say, 'It is an earthquake'; and sometimes they become quite furious with impatience, and then their fiery breath bursts through the mountains and puffs out molten iron and stones.

After the Giants were conquered, Gaea created a truly terrific being, far worse than they had been. She brought him out of a great crack that she made in the earth, and she called her son Typhöeus and was quite pleased to see how hideous he was, for she thought that such a monstrous creature would surely be able to conquer the young gods. He could see over the tops of the highest mountains, and when he stretched out his hands they reached right round the world. He had a hundred heads, each of them with a different kind of voice, so that he could speak like a man, bellow like a bull, roar like a lion, bark like a dog, and hiss like a snake. All the other gods were afraid of him and hid themselves, but Zeus armed himself with thunderbolts and went out to fight him. Typhöeus threw large masses of rock at him, and screamed with all his hundred mouths at once, but Zeus scorched him with lightning, till at last bright flames burst out all over the giant's body. Then Typhöeus howled and dashed himself to the ground, rolling over and over to try and put out the flames, but he could not succeed in doing so, for Zeus went on hurling thunderbolts at him, and the trees all round became red hot. At last Gaea began to fear that the whole earth would melt, and so she

seized Typhöeus and flung him down into Tartarus, where he died.

After this Gaea gave up fighting with the young
gods, for she knew that they were stronger than she
was, but it was a very long time before she really
made friends with them.

The Story of Prometheus

I. HOW FIRE WAS GIVEN TO MEN

In those old, old times, there lived two brothers who were not like other men, nor yet like those Mighty Ones who lived upon the mountain top. They were the sons of one of those Titans who had fought against Zeus and been sent in chains to the strong prison-house of the Lower World.

The name of the elder of these brothers was Prometheus, or Forethought; for he was always thinking of the future and making things ready for what might happen to-morrow, or next week, or next year, or it may be in a hundred years to come. The younger was called Epimetheus, or After-thought; for he was always so busy thinking of yesterday, or last year, or a hundred years ago, that he had no care at all for what might come to pass after a while.

For some cause Zeus had not sent these brothers to prison with the rest of the Titans.*

Prometheus did not care to live amid the clouds

---

* They had fought on the side of the Olympians during the war.

on the mountain top. He was too busy for that. While the Mighty Folk were spending their time in idleness, drinking nectar and eating ambrosia, he was intent upon plans for making the world wiser and better than it had ever been before.

He went out amongst men to live with them and help them; for his heart was filled with sadness when he found that they were no longer happy as they had been during the golden days when Saturn was king. Ah, how very poor and wretched they were! He found them living in caves and in holes of the earth, shivering with the cold because there was no fire, dying of starvation, hunted by wild beasts and by one another—the most miserable of all living creatures.

"If they only had fire," said Prometheus to himself, "they could at least warm themselves and cook their food; and after a while they could learn to make tools and build themselves houses. Without fire, they are worse off than the beasts."

Then he went boldly to Zeus and begged him to give fire to men, that so they might have a little comfort through the long, dreary months of winter.

"Not a spark will I give," said Zeus. "No, indeed! Why, if men had fire they might become strong and wise like ourselves, and after a while they would drive us out of our kingdom. Let them shiver with cold, and let them live like the beasts. It is best for them to be poor and ignorant, that so we Mighty Ones may thrive and be happy."

Prometheus made no answer; but he had set his heart on helping mankind, and he did not give up. He turned away, and left Zeus and his mighty company forever.

As he was walking by the shore of the sea he found a reed, or, as some say, a tall stalk of fennel, growing; and when he had broken it off he saw that its hollow center was filled with a dry, soft pith which would burn slowly and keep on fire a long time. He took the long stalk in his hands, and started with it towards the dwelling of the sun in the far east.

"Mankind shall have fire in spite of the tyrant who sits on the mountain top," he said.

He reached the place of the sun in the early morning just as the glowing, golden orb was rising from the earth and beginning his daily journey through the sky. He touched the end of the long reed to the flames, and the dry pith caught on fire and burned slowly. Then he turned and hastened back to his own land, carrying with him the precious spark hidden in the hollow center of the plant.

He called some of the shivering men from their

caves and built a fire for them, and showed them how to warm themselves by it and how to build other fires from the coals. Soon there was a cheerful blaze in every rude home in the land, and men and women gathered round it and were warm and happy, and thankful to Prometheus for the wonderful gift which he had brought to them from the sun.

It was not long until they learned to cook their food and so to eat like men instead of like beasts. They began at once to leave off their wild and savage habits; and instead of lurking in the dark places of the world, they came out into the open air and the bright sunlight, and were glad because life had been given to them.

After that, Prometheus taught them, little by little, a thousand things. He showed them how to build houses of wood and stone, and how to tame sheep and cattle and make them useful, and how to plow and sow and reap, and how to protect themselves from the storms of winter and the beasts of the woods. Then he showed them how to dig in the earth for copper and iron, and how to melt the ore, and how to hammer it into shape and fashion from it the tools and weapons which they needed in peace and war; and when he saw how happy the world was becoming he cried out:

"A new Golden Age shall come, brighter and better by far than the old!"

II. HOW DISEASES AND CARES CAME
AMONG MEN

Things might have gone on very happily indeed, and the Golden Age might really have come again, had it not been for Zeus. But one day, when he chanced to look down upon the earth, he saw the fires burning, and the people living in houses, and the flocks feeding on the hills, and the grain ripening in the fields, and this made him very angry.

"Who has done all this?" he asked.

And some one answered, "Prometheus!"

"What! that young Titan!" he cried. "Well, I will punish him in a way that will make him wish I had shut him up in the prison-house with his kinsfolk. But as for those puny men, let them keep their fire. I will make them ten times more miserable than they were before they had it."

Of course it would be easy enough to deal with Prometheus at any time, and so Zeus was in no great haste about it. He made up his mind to distress mankind first; and he thought of a plan for doing it in a very strange, roundabout way.

In the first place, he ordered his blacksmith Hephaestus, whose forge was in the crater of a burning mountain, to take a lump of clay which he gave him, and mold it into the form of a woman. Hephaestus did as he was bidden; and when he had finished the image, he carried it up to Zeus, who was sitting among the clouds with all the Mighty Folk around him. It was nothing but a mere lifeless body, but the great blacksmith had given it a form more perfect than that of any statue that has ever been made.

"Come now!" said Zeus, "let us all give some goodly gift to this woman;" and he began by giving her life.

Then the others came in their turn, each with a gift for the marvelous creature. One gave her beauty; and another a pleasant voice; and another good manners; and another a kind heart; and another skill in many arts; and, lastly, some one gave her curiosity. Then they called her Pandora, which means the all-gifted, because she had received gifts from them all.

Pandora was so beautiful and so wondrously gifted that no one could help loving her. When the Mighty Folk had admired her for a time, they gave her to Hermes, the light-footed; and he led her down the mountain side to the place where Prometheus and his brother were living and toiling for the good of mankind. He met Epimetheus first, and said to him:

"Epimetheus, here is a beautiful woman, whom Zeus has sent to you to be your wife."

Prometheus had often warned his brother to beware of any gift that Zeus might send, for he knew that the mighty tyrant could not be trusted; but when Epimetheus saw Pandora, how lovely and wise she was, he forgot all warnings, and took her home to live with him and be his wife.

Pandora was very happy in her new home; and even Prometheus, when he saw her, was pleased with her loveliness. She had brought with her a golden casket, which Zeus had given her at parting, and which he had told her held many precious things; but wise Athena, the queen of the air, had warned her never, never to open it, nor look at the things inside.*

"They must be jewels," she said to herself; and then she thought of how they would add to her beauty if only she could wear them. "Why did Zeus give them to me if I should never use them, nor so much as look at them?" she asked.

The more she thought about the golden casket,

---

* In Greek myth the object was a jar or vase as opposed to a casket or box.

the more curious she was to see what was in it; and every day she took it down from its shelf and felt of the lid, and tried to peer inside of it without opening it.

"Why should I care for what Athena told me?" she said at last. "She is not beautiful, and jewels would be of no use to her. I think that I will look at them, at any rate. Athena will never know. Nobody else will ever know."

She opened the lid a very little, just to peep inside. All at once there was a whirring, rustling sound, and before she could shut it down again, out flew ten thousand strange creatures with death-like faces and gaunt and dreadful forms, such as nobody in all the world had ever seen. They fluttered for a little while about the room, and then flew away to find dwelling-places wherever there were homes of men. They were diseases and cares; for up to that time mankind had not had any kind of sickness, nor felt any troubles of mind, nor worried about what the morrow might bring forth.

These creatures flew into every house, and, without any one seeing them, nestled down in the bosoms of men and women and children, and put an end to all their joy; and ever since that day they have been flitting and creeping, unseen and unheard, over all the land, bringing pain and sorrow and death into every household.

If Pandora had not shut down the lid so quickly, things would have gone much worse. But she closed it just in time to keep the last of the evil creatures from getting out. The name of this creature was Foreboding, and although he was almost half out of the casket, Pandora pushed him back and shut the lid so tight that he could never escape.* If he had gone out into the world, men would have known from childhood just what troubles were going to come to them every day of their lives, and they would never have had any joy or hope so long as they lived.

And this was the way in which Zeus sought to make mankind more miserable than they had been before Prometheus had befriended them.

III. HOW THE FRIEND OF MEN
WAS PUNISHED

The next thing that Zeus did was to punish Prometheus for stealing fire from the sun. He bade two of his servants, whose names were Strength and Force, to seize the bold Titan and carry him to the topmost peak of the Caucasus Mountains.

---

* The ancient version of this myth refers to hope not foreboding.

Then he sent the blacksmith Hephaestus to bind him with iron chains and fetter him to the rocks so that he could not move hand or foot.

Hephaestus did not like to do this, for he was a friend of Prometheus, and yet he did not dare to disobey. And so the great friend of men, who had given them fire and lifted them out of their wretchedness and shown them how to live, was chained to the mountain peak; and there he hung, with the storm-winds whistling always around him, and the pitiless hail beating in his face, and fierce eagles shrieking in his ears and tearing his body with their cruel claws. Yet he bore all his sufferings without a groan, and never would he beg for mercy or say that he was sorry for what he had done.

Year after year, and age after age, Prometheus hung there. Now and then old Helios, the driver of the sun car, would look down upon him and smile; now and then flocks of birds would bring him messages from far-off lands; once the ocean nymphs came and sang wonderful songs in his hearing; and oftentimes men looked up to him with pitying eyes, and cried out against the tyrant who had placed him there.

Then, once upon a time, a white cow passed that way,—a strangely beautiful cow, with large sad eyes and a face that seemed almost human. She stopped and looked up at the cold gray peak and the giant body which was chained there. Prometheus saw her and spoke to her kindly:

"I know who you are," he said. "You are Io who was once a fair and happy maiden in distant Argos; and now, because of the tyrant Zeus and his jealous queen, you are doomed to wander from land to land in that unhuman form. But do not lose hope. Go on to the southward and then to the west; and after many days you shall come to the great river Nile. There you shall again become a maiden, but fairer and more beautiful than before; and you shall become the wife of the king of that land, and shall give birth to a son, from whom shall spring the hero who will break my chains and set me free. As for me, I bide in patience the day which not even Zeus can hasten or delay. Farewell!"

Poor Io would have spoken, but she could not. Her sorrowful eyes looked once more at the suffering hero on the peak, and then she turned and began her long and tiresome journey to the land of the Nile.

Ages passed, and at last a great hero whose name was Heracles came to the land of the Caucasus. In spite of Zeus's dread thunderbolts and fearful storms of snow and sleet, he climbed the rugged mountain peak; he slew the fierce eagles that had so long tormented the helpless prisoner on those craggy heights; and with a mighty blow, he broke the fetters of Prometheus and set the grand old hero free.

"I knew that you would come," said Prometheus. "Ten generations ago I spoke of you to Io, who was afterwards the queen of the land of the Nile."

"And Io," said Heracles, "was the mother of the race from which I am sprung."

The Deluge

≈≈≈≈≈≈≈≈≈≈

After disease and care had come into the world, men became unkind and unfriendly; instead of peace there was now constant war, and murder and theft were more common every day. The gods were much displeased at these crimes, and Zeus said he would destroy the whole race of men by a great flood. There were, however, one man and one woman, Deucalion and Pyrrha, who took no part in the crimes that were committed, but who lived peacefully and uprightly, fearing the gods. Deucalion was the son of Prometheus, who knew everything that the gods had resolved upon though he was chained to Mount Caucasus, and when the great flood was about to take place, he advised Deucalion to provide against it by building a chest that could float on the water, so that when the flood began, he and his wife might take shelter in it.

Then a mighty rain poured down from heaven which lasted for nine days and nine nights. The valleys were soon filled with water, and the people fled for safety to the tops of the highest mountains; but the flood rose higher and higher till at last the waves washed right over the mountains, so that the people perished miserably in the water. The great chest floated about on the top of the waves, and Deucalion and Pyrrha who were safely shut up inside it, could hear the pouring rain and the cries of the drowning people. When they were all drowned, the rain ceased and the waters began to abate, and on the next day the bottom of the chest grated against dry land. Then Deucalion burst it open, and he and Pyrrha came out into the sunshine, but all they could see was a wide stretch of sea with only the tops of the highest mountains standing out above it. The mountain where the chest had stranded was called Parnassus, and was specially dedicated to the gods. Before this time Zeus had once wanted to know where the middle of the earth was, and had let fly two doves at the same moment from the two ends of the world to see where they would meet: they met on Mount Parnassus, and thus it was proved beyond a doubt, that this mountain must be the centre of the earth.

Deucalion and Pyrrha were now the only ones remaining of the whole human race, and it was on account of their piety that Zeus had allowed them to save themselves instead of destroying them with the others. The waters abated until they no longer covered the earth, and then the grass and flowers and trees bloomed forth again as they do in spring, and Zeus sent Hermes, the messenger of the gods, to tell Deucalion and Pyrrha that they might ask for anything they pleased, and he would grant it. They determined to ask that there might again be men on the earth, and Hermes told them to go into the valley where there were a great many stones lying, and to take up the stones and throw them over their shoulders. They did so, and this was what happened: every stone that Deucalion threw became a man, and every stone that Pyrrha threw became a woman. Deucalion was their king, and he taught them to cultivate the land, and many other useful arts. And after some time had passed the whole earth was filled with people as before, and no one would have known that the great Flood had ever taken place.

THE LIVES OF THE GODS

After the third generation of gods and goddesses defeated the Titans and Zeus was appointed their king, they went on to have their own sons and daughters who joined them on Olympus. Each deity ruled over their own domain and was revered by the people on earth, yet life on Olympus was hardly harmonious. The gods and goddesses of ancient Greek myth continued to bicker and compete, whether over lovers, power, or even herds of cows. Here you will find just a few of the tales that survive about the lives of the Greek gods and goddesses. From outlandish accounts of their births to tales of their contentious relationships, the writers collected here offer readers a glimpse of the world of deities so widely revered by the ancient Greeks.

Poseidon and the Sea-Gods

In the days when the Titans ruled the universe, Oceanus, with his wife Tethys, controlled all the lakes, rivers, and seas; but when the Titans were overthrown, Poseidon took possession of this great kingdom, and old Oceanus reluctantly gave up his dominion over the waters of the earth. Though anxious to assert his supreme authority, Poseidon allowed some of the descendants of the Titans to keep their small kingdoms, on condition that they own allegiance to him as their ruler. Among these was Nereus, son of Oceanus, who was celebrated for his vast knowledge, his gift of prophecy, and his love of truth and justice. He and his wife Doris (also a child of Oceanus) had fifty daughters called Nereids, and they were so beautiful that Poseidon chose one of them, named Amphitrite, for his wife. There were two others of the Nereids who became famous: Galatea, beloved by the Cyclops Polyphemus, and Thetis, the mother of Achilles; but none of them equaled Amphitrite in beauty.

When Poseidon first went wooing the Nereid,

she was frightened by his formidable appearance, for he drove in a chariot drawn by huge sea-horses with brazen hoofs and golden manes; and the god himself carried his terrible trident, or three-pronged spear, with which he shatters rocks, and commands the storms, and shakes the shores of earth. None knew better than Amphitrite the extent of Poseidon's power, for she had often watched him, when a storm was at its height, raise his all-compelling trident, and immediately the waves would cease raging and there would be a great calm. Sometimes she saw a ship, doomed by the sea-god to disaster, gliding confidently in quiet waters, when all at once a fierce storm would break over its head; and the hapless sailors, as they breasted the angry waves, would pray vainly to Poseidon for the help that would never come. Many a good ship had nearly gained her port when

> "He spake and round about him called the clouds
> And roused the ocean—wielding in his hand
> The trident—summoned all the hurricanes
> Of all the winds, and covered earth and sky
> At once with mists, while from above the night
> Fell suddenly."
>
> —*ODYSSEY*, Book V, line 348, tr. William Cullen Bryant.

When Amphitrite saw this imposing-looking god driving toward her, she was frightened by so much splendor, though she could not help admiring Poseidon himself with his sea-green beard, and his long flowing hair crowned with shells and seaweed. Since the enamored god could never come near enough to plead his suit, he sent one of his dolphins to do the wooing; and this was so successful that the fair Nereid was persuaded to become Poseidon's wife, and share his golden throne in the heart of the sea. To reward the dolphin for its skill in having won for him his much-desired bride, Poseidon placed it in the sky, where it forms a well-known constellation.

Though Poseidon had undisputed control over all the waters of the earth, and over all that moves through the paths of the sea, he once aspired to greater power, and even plotted to dethrone Zeus. But the ruler of gods and men discovered his wicked plans, and to punish him deprived him of his kingdom for some years, during which time he was obliged to submit to the humiliation of serving Laomedon, king of Troy. It was while he was in service here that he sought Apollo's help in building the wall of Troy, whose stones fell into place under the spell of the sun-god's music. Laomedon had promised Poseidon a large reward if the wall was built within a certain time; but when it was finished, he refused to pay the sum agreed upon. Though angered at this treachery, Poseidon had to endure the king's injustice until his years of service were over; but as soon as he was restored to his former power, he created a terrible sea-monster, which spread terror and death over all the land. Not knowing how to meet this calamity, the Trojans consulted an oracle, and were advised to sacrifice to the monster a beautiful maiden each year; and so prevent the wrath of Poseidon from overwhelming the whole country in disaster.

Reluctantly the sorrowing people prepared to obey the oracle; and a victim was chosen by lot, and led by the priest to a large rock on the sea-shore, where she was securely chained. Then the hideous sea-beast glided out of its cave in the slimy rocks and devoured her. Each year this terrible ceremony was repeated, and at last the lot fell upon Hesione, the king's only daughter. Laomedon tried in vain to save her, but the lot was cast, and nothing could avert the appointed sacrifice. In despair, the wretched father saw the fatal hour approaching; and when the day drew near when Hesione was to be led down to the sea, he forgot his avarice and proclaimed throughout the land that a great reward would be given to any one who could slay the monster. Heracles appeared just in time to save the doomed maiden, and killed the monster with his oaken club as it was dragging Hesione into its cave. The king was overjoyed at his daughter's rescue, and told Heracles that he might claim the reward; but even when he saw the hero come with the beast's head as a proof that he had slain it, he refused to part with his much-loved gold. So Heracles returned home, but he did not forget Laomedon's perfidy; and when later on he came again to Troy, he killed the king and took his children captive to Greece.

Poseidon, like all the immortals, loved more than once; and among those who shared his affections was a maiden named Theophane, who had so many suitors that it kept the jealous sea-god in constant fear lest she should prefer some earthly lover. So he took her to the island of Crumissa, and there changed her into a sheep, while he carried on his wooing in the form of a ram. The offspring of this marriage was the famous golden-fleeced ram, whose pelt was the object of that ill-fated expedition made by Jason and his fellow Argonauts.

Poseidon also loved the goddess Demeter, and followed her during the long time that she spent in search of her daughter Persephone. Demeter was angered by the sea-god's persistent wooing, and hoping to escape from him, she took the form of a mare; but Poseidon was not so easily discouraged, for he changed himself into a horse and contentedly trotted after her. The child of this strange pair was Arion, a wonderful winged steed that had the power of speech, and was of such incredible swiftness that nothing could ever equal it in speed.

The most famous children of Poseidon and Amphitrite were Triton and Proteus. Triton was his father's trumpeter, and at Poseidon's command he blew upon his conch-shell to calm the restless sea. His body was half man and half fish, and he gave the name of Tritons to all his male descendants, who, with the Nereids and Oceanides (daughters of Oceanus), followed the chariot of Poseidon when he went abroad to view his kingdom. Proteus had charge of the great flock of sea-calves which fed on the soft seaweed and basked in the warm sands near his cave. He was celebrated for his wisdom and for the truth of the answers that he gave to those fortunate enough to make him speak. Homer calls him "the Ancient of the Deep whose words are ever true"; but his knowledge was not easy to obtain, for he had the extraordinary power of assuming any shape he pleased, and only those mortals gained his advice who persistently clung to him through his many bewildering changes.

Athena

THE BIRTH OF ATHENA

Although immortal, the gods were not exempt from physical pain. One day Zeus suffered intensely from a sudden headache, and, in hopes that some mode of alleviation would be devised, he summoned all the gods to Olympus. Their united efforts were vain, however; and even the remedies suggested by Apollo, god of medicine, proved inefficacious. Unwilling, or perchance unable, to endure the racking pain any longer, Zeus bade one of his sons, Hephaestus, cleave his head open with an axe. With cheerful alacrity the dutiful god obeyed; and no sooner was the operation performed, than Athena (Pallas, Athene) sprang out of her father's head, full-grown, clad in glittering armour, with poised spear, and chanting a triumphant song of victory.

> "From his awful head
> Whom Jove [Zeus] brought forth, in warlike
>   armour drest,
> Golden, all radiant."
>   —SHELLEY.

The assembled gods recoiled in fear before this unexpected apparition, while at the same time a mighty commotion over land and sea proclaimed the advent of a great divinity.

The goddess, who had thus joined the inhabitants of Olympus, was destined to preside over peace, defensive war, and needlework, to be the incarnation of wisdom, and to put to flight the obscure deity called Dulness, who until then had ruled the world.*

"Ere Pallas issu'd from the Thund'rer's head,
Dulness o'er all possess'd her ancient right,
Daughter of Chaos and eternal Night."
—POPE.

THE CLASSICAL MYTHS

Athena, having forced her unattractive predecessor to beat an ignominious retreat, quickly seized the sceptre and immediately began to rule in her stead.

Not long after her birth, Cecrops, a Phœnician, came to Greece, where he founded a beautiful city in the province since called Attica. All the gods watched his undertaking with great interest; and

* Dulness is an invention of the writer Alexander Pope rather than a real ancient Greek goddess.

finally, seeing the town promised to become a thriving place, each wished the privilege of naming it. A general council was held, and after some deliberation most of the gods withdrew their claims. Soon none but Athena and Poseidon were left to contend for the coveted honour.

To settle the quarrel without evincing any partiality, Zeus announced that the city would be entrusted to the protection of the deity who would create the most useful object for the use of man. Raising his trident, Poseidon struck the ground, from which a noble horse sprang forth, amid the exclamations of wonder and admiration of all the spectators.* His qualities were duly explained by his proud creator, and all thought it quite impossible for Athena to surpass him. Loudly they laughed, and scornfully too, when she, in her turn, produced an olive tree; but when she had told them the manifold uses to which wood, fruit, foliage, twigs, &c., could be applied, and explained that the olive was the sign of peace and prosperity, and therefore far more desirable than the horse, the emblem of war and wretchedness, they could but acknowledge her gift the most serviceable, and award her the prize.

* In most ancient versions Poseidon gifts the mortals with a spring.

To commemorate this victory over her rival, Athena gave her name to the city, whose inhabitants, from that time forth, were taught to honour her as their tutelary goddess.

Ever at Zeus's side, Athena often aided him by her wise counsels, and in times of war borrowed his terrible shield, the Ægis, which she flung over her shoulder when she sallied forth to give her support to those whose cause was just.

The din of battle had no terrors for this doughty goddess, and on every occasion she was wont to plunge into the thickest of the fray with the utmost valour.

Hephaestus

ᒫᒫᒫᒫᒫᒫᒫᒫᒫ

Vulcan, or Hephaestus, son of Zeus and Hera, god of fire and the forge, seldom joined the general council of the gods. His aversion to Olympus was of old standing. He had once been tenderly attached to his mother, had lavished upon her every proof of his affection, and had even tried to console her when she mourned Zeus's neglect. On one occasion, intending to punish Hera for one of her usual fits of jealousy, Zeus hung her out of heaven, fast bound by a golden chain; and Hephaestus, perceiving her in this plight, tugged at the chain with all his might, drew her up, and was about to set her free, when Zeus returned, and, in anger at his son's interference in his matrimonial concerns, kicked him out of heaven.

The intervening space between heaven and earth was so great, that Hephaestus's fall lasted during one whole day and night, ere he finally touched the summit of Mount Mosychlus, in the Island of Lemnos.

Of course, to anyone but a god such a terrible fall would have proved fatal; and even Hephaestus did not escape entirely unharmed, for he damaged one of his legs, which left him permanently injured.

Now, although Hephaestus had risked so much and suffered so greatly in taking his mother's part, she never even made the slightest attempt to ascertain whether he had reached the earth in safety. Hurt by her indifference and ingratitude, Hephaestus vowed never again to return to Olympus, and withdrew to the solitudes of Mount Etna, where he established a great forge in the heart of the mountain, in partnership with the Cyclopes, who helped him manufacture many cunning and useful objects from the metals found in great profusion in the bosom of the earth.

Among these ingenious contrivances were two golden handmaidens gifted with motion, who attended the god wherever he went, and supported his halting footsteps.

Hephaestus also devised a golden throne with countless hidden springs, which, when unoccupied, did not present an extraordinary appearance; but as soon as any one ventured to make use of it, the springs moved, and, the chair closing around the person seated upon it, frustrated all attempts to rise and escape from its treacherous embrace.

Hephaestus dispatched this throne, when completed, to his mother, who, delighted with its beauty and delicate workmanship, proudly seated herself upon it, and found herself a prisoner. In vain she strove to escape, in vain the gods all gallantly rushed to her assistance. Their united strength and skill proved useless against the cunning springs.

Finally Hermes was sent to Hephaestus, primed with a most diplomatic request to honor high Olympus with his presence; but all Hermes's eloquence and persuasions failed to induce the god of the forge to leave his sooty abode, and the messenger god was forced to return alone and report the failure of his attempt. Then the gods deliberated anew, and decided to send Dionysus, god of wine, hoping his powers of persuasion would prove more effective.

Armed with a flask of his choicest vintage, Dionysus presented himself before Hephaestus, and offered him a refreshing draught. Hephaestus, predisposed to thirst, and incited to drink by the very nature of his labor, accepted the offered cup, and allowed himself to be beguiled into renewing his potations, until he was quite intoxicated. In this condition, Dionysus led him passive to Olympus, made him release the Queen of Heaven, and urged him to embrace his father and crave forgiveness.

Although restored to favor, Hephaestus would not remain permanently in Olympus, but preferred to return to his forge and continue his labors. He undertook, however, the construction of magnificent golden palaces for each of the gods upon the Olympian heights, fashioned their sumptuous furniture from precious metals, and further embellished his work by a rich ornamentation of precious stones.

The Lord of the Silver Bow

Long before you or I or anybody else can remember, there lived with the Mighty Folk on the mountain top a fair and gentle lady named Leto. So fair and gentle was she that Zeus loved her and made her his wife. But when Hera, the queen of earth and sky, heard of this, she was very angry; and she drove Leto down from the mountain and bade all things great and small refuse to help her. So Leto fled like a wild deer from land to land and could find no place in which to rest. She could not stop, for then the ground would quake under her feet, and the stones would cry out, "Go on! go on!" and birds and beasts and trees and men would join in the cry; and no one in all the wide land took pity on her.

One day she came to the sea, and as she fled along the beach she lifted up her hands and called aloud to great Poseidon to help her. Poseidon, the king of the sea, heard her and was kind to her. He sent a huge fish, called a dolphin, to bear her away from the cruel land; and the fish, with Leto sitting

43

on his broad back, swam through the waves to Delos, a little island which lay floating on top of the water like a boat. There the gentle lady found rest and a home; for the place belonged to Poseidon, and the words of cruel Hera were not obeyed there. Poseidon put four marble pillars under the island so that it should rest firm upon them; and then he chained it fast, with great chains which reached to the bottom of the sea, so that the waves might never move it.

By and by twin babes were born to Leto in Delos. One was a boy whom she called Apollo, the other a girl whom she named Artemis, or Diana. When the news of their birth was carried to Zeus and the Mighty Folk on the mountain top, all the world was glad. The sun danced on the waters, and singing swans flew seven times round the island of Delos. The moon stooped to kiss the babes in their cradle; and Hera forgot her anger, and bade all things on the earth and in the sky be kind to Leto.

The two children grew very fast. Apollo became tall and strong and graceful; his face was as bright as the sunbeams; and he carried joy and gladness with him wherever he went. Zeus gave him a pair of swans and a golden chariot, which bore him over sea and land wherever he wanted to go; and he gave him a lyre on which he played the sweetest music that was ever heard, and a silver bow with sharp arrows which never missed the mark. When Apollo went out into the world, and men came to know about him, he was called by some the Bringer of Light, by others the Master of Song, and by still others the Lord of the Silver Bow.

Artemis was tall and graceful, too, and very handsome. She liked to wander in the woods with her maids, who were called nymphs; she took kind care of the timid deer and the helpless creatures which live among the trees; and she delighted in hunting wolves and bears and other savage beasts. She was loved and feared in every land, and Zeus made her the queen of the green woods and the chase.

DELPHI

"Where is the center of the world?"

This is the question which some one asked Zeus as he sat in his golden hall. Of course the mighty ruler of earth and sky was too wise to be puzzled by so simple a thing, but he was too busy to answer it at once. So he said:

"Come again in one year from to-day, and I will show you the very place."

Then Zeus took two swift eagles which could fly faster than the storm-wind, and trained them till

45

the speed of the one was the same as that of the other. At the end of the year he said to his servants:

"Take this eagle to the eastern rim of the earth, where the sun rises out of the sea; and carry his fellow to the far west, where the ocean is lost in darkness and nothing lies beyond. Then, when I give you the sign, loosen both at the same moment."

The servants did as they were bidden, and carried the eagles to the outermost edges of the world. Then Zeus clapped his hands. The lightning flashed, the thunder rolled, and the two swift birds were set free. One of them flew straight back towards the west, the other flew straight back towards the east; and no arrow ever sped faster from the bow than did these two birds from the hands of those who had held them.

On and on they went like shooting stars rushing to meet each other; and Zeus and all his mighty company sat amid the clouds and watched their flight. Nearer and nearer they came, but they swerved not to the right nor to the left. Nearer and nearer—and then with a crash like the meeting of two ships at sea, the eagles came together in mid-air and fell dead to the ground.

"Who asked where is the center of the world?" said Zeus. "The spot where the two eagles lie—that is the center of the world."

They had fallen on the top of a mountain in Greece which men have ever since called Parnassus.

"If that is the center of the world," said young Apollo, "then I will make my home there, and I will build a house in that place, so that my light may be seen in all lands."

So Apollo went down to Parnassus, and looked about for a spot in which to lay the foundations of his house. The mountain itself was savage and wild, and the valley below it was lonely and dark. The few people who lived there kept themselves hidden among the rocks as if in dread of some great danger. They told Apollo that near the foot of the mountain where the steep cliff seemed to be split in two there lived a huge serpent called the Python. This serpent often seized sheep and cattle, and sometimes even men and women and children, and carried them up to his dreadful den and devoured them.

"Can no one kill this beast?" said Apollo.

And they said, "No one; and we and our children and our flocks shall all be slain by him."

Then Apollo with his silver bow in his hands went up towards the place where the Python lay. The monster had worn great paths through the grass and among the rocks, and his lair was not hard to find. When he caught sight of Apollo, he uncoiled himself, and came out to meet him. The bright prince saw the creature's glaring eyes and blood-red mouth, and heard the rush of his scaly body over the stones. He fitted an arrow to his bow, and stood still. The Python saw that his foe was no common man, and turned to flee. Then the arrow sped from the bow—and the monster was dead.

"Here I will build my house," said Apollo.

Close to the foot of the steep cliff, and beneath the spot where Zeus's eagles had fallen, he laid the foundations; and soon where had been the lair of the Python, the white walls of Apollo's temple arose among the rocks. Then the poor people of the land came and built their houses near by; and Apollo lived among them many years, and taught them to be gentle and wise, and showed them how to be happy. The mountain was no longer savage and wild, but was a place of music and song; the valley was no longer dark and lonely, but was filled with beauty and light.

"What shall we call our city?" the people asked.

"Call it Delphi, or the Dolphin," said Apollo; "for it was a dolphin that carried my mother across the sea."

Apollo did not care to live much of the time with his mighty kinsfolk on the mountain top. He liked better to go about from place to place and from land to land, seeing people at their work and making their lives happy. When men first saw his fair boyish face and his soft white hands, they sneered and said he was only an idle, good-for-nothing fellow. But when they heard him speak, they were so charmed that they stood, spellbound, to listen; and ever after that they made his words their law. They wondered how it was that he was so wise; for it seemed to them that he did nothing but stroll about, playing on his wonderful lyre and looking at the trees and blossoms and birds and bees. But when any of them were sick they came to him, and he told them what to find in plants or stones or brooks that would heal them and make them strong again. They noticed that he did not grow old, as others did, but that he was always young and fair; and, even after he had gone away,— they knew not how, nor whither,—it seemed as though the earth were a brighter and sweeter place to live in than it had been before his coming.

In a mountain village beyond the Vale of Tempe, there lived a beautiful lady named Coronis. When Apollo saw her, he loved her and made her his wife; and for a long time the two lived together, and were happy. By and by a babe was born to them,—a boy with the most wonderful eyes that anybody ever saw,—and they named him Æsculapius. Then the mountains and the woods were filled with the music of Apollo's lyre, and even the Mighty Folk on the mountain top were glad.

One day Apollo left Coronis and her child, and went on a journey to visit his favorite home on Mount Parnassus.

"I shall hear from you every day," he said at parting. "The crow will fly swiftly every morning to Parnassus, and tell me whether you and the child are well, and what you are doing while I am away."

For Apollo had a pet crow which was very wise, and could talk. The bird was not black, like the crows which you have seen, but as white as snow. Men say that all crows were white until that time, but I doubt whether anybody knows.

Apollo's crow was a great tattler, and did not always tell the truth. It would see the beginning of something, and then, without waiting to know anything more about it, would hurry off and make up a great story about it. But there was no one else to carry news from Coronis to Apollo; for, as you know, there were no postmen in those days, and there was not a telegraph wire in the whole world.

50

All went well for several days. Every morning the white bird would wing its way over hills and plains and rivers and forests until it found Apollo, either in the groves on the top of Parnassus or in his own house at Delphi. Then it would alight upon his shoulder and say, "Coronis is well! Coronis is well!"

One day, however, it had a different story. It came much earlier than ever before, and seemed to be in great haste.

"Cor—Cor—Cor!" it cried; but it was so out of breath that it could not speak her whole name.

"What is the matter?" cried Apollo, in alarm. "Has anything happened to Coronis? Speak! Tell me the truth!"

"She does not love you! she does not love you!" cried the crow. "I saw a man—I saw a man,—" and then, without stopping to take breath, or to finish the story, it flew up into the air, and hurried homeward again.

Apollo, who had always been so wise, was now almost as foolish as his crow. He fancied that Coronis had really deserted him for another man, and his mind was filled with grief and rage. With his silver bow in his hands he started at once for his home. He did not stop to speak with any one; he had made up his mind to learn the truth for himself. His swan-team and his golden chariot were not at hand—for, now that he was living with men, he must travel like men. The journey had to be made on foot, and it was no short journey in those days when there were no roads. But after a time, he came to the village where he had lived happily for so many years, and soon he saw his own house half hidden among the dark-leaved olive trees. In another minute he would know whether the crow had told him the truth.

He heard the footsteps of some one running in the grove. He caught a glimpse of a white robe among the trees. He felt sure that this was the man whom the crow had seen, and that he was trying to run away. He fitted an arrow to his bow quickly. He drew the string. Twang! And the arrow which never missed sped like a flash of light through the air.

Apollo heard a sharp, wild cry of pain; and he bounded forward through the grove. There, stretched dying on the grass, he saw his dear Coronis. She had seen him coming, and was running gladly to greet him, when the cruel arrow pierced her heart. Apollo was overcome with grief. He took her form in his arms, and tried to call her back to life again. But it was all in vain. She could only whisper his name, and then she was dead.

A moment afterwards the crow alighted on one

of the trees near by. "Cor—Cor—Cor," it began; for it wanted now to finish its story. But Apollo bade it begone.

"Cursed bird," he cried, "you shall never say a word but 'Cor—Cor—Cor!' all your life; and the feathers of which you are so proud shall no longer be white, but black as midnight."

And from that time to this, as you very well know, all crows have been black; and they fly from one dead tree to another, always crying, "Cor—cor—cor!"

DISGRACED

Soon after this, Apollo took the little Æsculapius in his arms and carried him to a wise old school-master named Cheiron, who lived in a cave under the gray cliffs of a mountain close by the sea.

"Take this child," he said, "and teach him all the lore of the mountains, the woods, and the fields. Teach him those things which he most needs to know in order to do great good to his fellow-men."

And Æsculapius proved to be a wise child, gentle and sweet and teachable; and among all the pupils of Cheiron he was the best loved. He learned the lore of the mountains, the woods, and the fields. He found out what virtue there is in herbs and flowers and senseless stones; and he studied the habits of birds and beasts and men. But above all he became skillful in dressing wounds and healing diseases; and to this day physicians remember and honor him as the first and greatest of their craft. When he grew up to manhood his name was heard in every land, and people blessed him because he was the friend of life and the foe of death.

As time went by, Æsculapius cured so many people and saved so many lives that Hades, the pale-faced king of the Lower World, became alarmed.

"I shall soon have nothing to do," he said, "if this physician does not stop keeping people away from my kingdom."

And he sent word to his brother Zeus, and complained that Æsculapius was cheating him out of what was his due. Great Zeus listened to his complaint, and stood up among the storm clouds, and hurled his thunderbolts at Æsculapius until the great physician was cruelly slain. Then all the world was filled with grief, and even the beasts and the trees and the stones wept because the friend of life was no more.

When Apollo heard of the death of his son, his grief and wrath were terrible. He could not do anything against Zeus and Hades, for they were stronger than he; but he went down into the smithy of Hephaestus, underneath the smoking mountains, and slew the giant smiths who had made the deadly thunderbolts.

Then Zeus, in his turn, was angry, and ordered Apollo to come before him and be punished for what he had done. He took away his bow and arrows and his wonderful lyre and all his beauty of form and feature; and after that Zeus clothed him in the rags of a beggar and drove him down from the mountain, and told him that he should never come back nor be himself again until he had served some man a whole year as a slave.

And so Apollo went out, alone and friendless, into the world; and no one who saw him would have dreamed that he was once the sun-bright Lord of the Silver Bow.

The Story of Persephone

~~~~~~~~~~

When Zeus made himself ruler of the world, he imprisoned some of the warring giants under Mount Etna in Sicily, much to the disgust of Hades, who was always fearing that when the giants got restless and turned over and over underground (thus causing earthquakes), they would some day make such a large crack in the earth that daylight would be let into Hades. So Hades often went up out of his sunless land to look carefully over the island, and to be sure that no new fissure was being made in the earth's surface. One day, as he was driving his four coal-black horses through the vale of Enna, he saw a group of maidens gathering violets on the hillside; and among them was one so exquisitely fair that Hades determined to take her for his wife. This was Persephone, daughter of Demeter, the goddess of agriculture, a maiden who had ever shunned the thought of marriage and preferred to spend her life playing games, and dancing in the beautiful plain of Enna, where there is never any frost or snow, but springtime lasts through all the year.

Hades had often tried to gain a wife by gentle means, but no one would consent to share his grewsome home; so, knowing that this maiden he desired would never listen to soft words of love, he determined to take her by force. Driving his fiery horses at full speed, he rushed toward the group of laughing girls, who scattered and fled at his approach. Persephone alone stood still, and stared, frightened and wondering, at the grim figure confronting her, while the flowers she had gathered dropped from her trembling hands. In a moment Hades had seized her in his strong arms; and, trampling all her violets under his ruthless feet, he sprang into the chariot and urged his horses to their full speed, hoping to reach Hades before the maiden's cries brought Demeter to the rescue.

As he neared the Cyane River the waters, wishing to befriend Persephone, began to rise higher and higher, and with tossing waves opposed the madly-rushing steeds. Fearing to risk the chariot in the angry waters, Hades struck the ground with his terrible two-pronged fork, and a great chasm opened before him, into which the ruler of Hades hurriedly plunged. Then the earth closed again over him and the captured maiden. During the dreadful moments when Persephone felt herself held a prisoner in the arms of this bold wooer, she called wildly to her mother for help; but soon she realized that her cries would never reach Demeter's ears, and that she must find some other way to let the goddess know of her unhappy fate. So she summoned enough strength to struggle in her captor's embrace until she freed one arm from his hold, and with it loosened her girdle, which she flung into the Cyane River just before the yawning earth hid her so completely that no traces were left to tell where she had gone.

When Demeter came that evening into the vale of Enna and found that her daughter was not playing as usual with the other maidens, she questioned them, and learned their tearful story of the chariot with its four black horses and terrible driver. Just what had become of Persephone no one could tell her; so the distracted mother began her search, not knowing whether she might at any moment come upon her daughter's body mangled by the chariot wheels. For days and days she wandered, never stopping to rest except for a few hours at night when it was too dark for her to see her way. Rosy-fingered Eos, when she left her soft couch to open the gates of the morning, and Hesperus, when he led out the stars at evening, saw her still searching for the lost Persephone. Sometimes she was so weary that she sank down by the roadside and let the night-dew drench her aching limbs. Sometimes she rested under the trees when a storm broke over her head; but even here the rain beat down upon her, and the wind blew its cold breath in her face. Kindly people gave her food whenever she stopped to ask for it, and though none knew that she was a goddess, they sympathized with her grief when she told them that she was seeking her lost child. Only once did she meet with unkindness. She was sitting at a cottage door eating gruel from a bowl, and a lad—Stellio by name—laughed insolently at her enjoyment of the meal. To punish him for his rudeness the goddess threw some of the gruel in his face, and immediately he was changed into a lizard.

One day Demeter found herself near the city of Eleusis, and to avoid being recognized as a goddess, she disguised herself as an old beggar woman. She sat for a long time on a stone by the roadside, mourning her lost Persephone, until a little girl came by, driving some goats. Seeing the old woman's tearful face, the child stopped to ask her her trouble, but before Demeter could answer, the girl's father joined her and together they begged the stranger to come to their cottage and rest. The goddess yielded at last to their kindly insistence, and as she walked beside the old man, whose name was Celeus, he told her that at home he had a sick boy who had lately grown so ill that to-day they believed he would surely die. Demeter listened to his pathetic story, and for a moment forgot her own grief. Seeing a chance to return the old man's kindness, she followed him into the cottage; but first stopped by the meadow to gather a handful of poppies. When the parents led her to the sick child's bedside, she stooped and kissed the pale little face and immediately it became rosy with health. The boy sprang up well and strong again, to the great astonishment of his delighted family.

As they sat at the simple evening meal, the goddess put some poppy-juice in the glass of milk set out for the boy; and that night, when he was in a heavy sleep, she rubbed his body with oil, murmured over him a solemn charm, and was about to lay him on the red-hot ashes in the fire—that his mortal parts might be consumed and he himself be made immortal—when his mother chanced to enter the room, and springing forward with a cry of horror, snatched the boy from the fire. Before the excited mother could vent her wrath on the old woman, Demeter assumed her goddess form and quietly reproved the intruder; for her interference had not averted a harm, but had prevented a great gift from being conferred upon the unconscious child.

When Demeter left the cottage of Celeus, she continued her wanderings over the earth, and finally returned, discouraged and heartbroken, to Sicily. Chancing to be near the river Cyane, she went down to the water's edge to drink, and happily discovered the girdle that Persephone had dropped there in her flight. This made her hopeful of finding further traces of her lost daughter, so she lingered by the river bank, eagerly scanning the overflowing stream. As she stood there holding the recovered girdle in her hand, she heard a low murmuring sound as if some one were speaking in whispers. The goddess listened, wondering from what place the voice came; and soon she found that the soft tones proceeded from a fountain which was so close to her that its lightly-tossed spray fell on her hand. The murmur was often indistinct, but Demeter understood enough to realize that the words were addressed to her, and that the fountain was trying to tell her how Hades had come up from Hades and carried off Persephone to be his wife.

While the goddess was musing over this painful revelation, the fountain went on to say that it had not always been a stream in sunny Sicily, but was once a maiden named Arethusa and a native of the country of Elis. As a follower of Artemis she had roamed the wooded hills; and one day, being wearied from the chase, she sought refreshment in the forest stream. The drooping willows hung protectingly over the water, and here the nymph bathed fearlessly, believing herself alone. But Alpheus, the river-god, heard the splashing of the water, and rose from his grassy bed to see who was disturbing his noon-day rest. At the sight of Arethusa he was so delighted that he ventured to approach her; but she fled terrified through the forest, calling on Artemis for help. The goddess, hearing her cries, changed her into a fountain; and to further baffle the pursuing Alpheus, she wrapped it in a thick mist. As the river-god could no longer see the nymph, he was about to give up the chase, when Zephyrus maliciously blew away the cloud, and Alpheus saw the bubbling fountain. Suspecting that this was Arethusa, the god changed himself into a rushing torrent, and was preparing to mingle his impetuous waves with the waters of the fountain, when the nymph again called on Artemis to protect her. The goddess came to her rescue by opening a crevice in the earth, and here the shivering waters of the fountain found a speedy refuge. To keep far out of the reach of Alpheus it continued to flow underground for many miles, and even crept beneath the sea until it reached Sicily, where Artemis again cleft the earth and allowed the fountain to come up into the sunlight. During her journey through the dark underworld, Arethusa said that she had seen Persephone sitting, tearful and sad, on a throne beside the grim ruler of the dead.

When she heard this story, Demeter was no longer in doubt where her lost daughter could be found; but the knowledge gave her little comfort, for she was aware how useless it would be to ask Hades to give up the wife he had so daringly won. Seeing no hope of regaining her child, Demeter retired to a cave in the hills, and paid no heed to the waiting earth that had suffered so long from her neglect. There was drought in the land, and the crops were failing for want of water. The fruit trees were drying up, and the flowers were withering on the parched hillsides. Everything cried out for the protecting care of Demeter; but the goddess stayed her hand, and in the solitude of the cave mourned unceasingly for Persephone. Famine spread over the land, but the people, in spite of their dire need of food, burned sacrifices of sheep and oxen on the altars of Demeter, while they importuned her with their prayers. Zeus heard their cries and besought the goddess to take the earth again under her wise care; but Demeter refused to listen, for she was indifferent now to the welfare of men, and no longer delighted in the ripening harvest.

When sickness and death followed hard upon the famine, Zeus saw that he must save the sorely-stricken land, so he promised the goddess that her daughter should be restored to her if she had eaten nothing during all her sojourn in Hades's realm. Hermes was sent to lead Persephone out of Hades; but when he reached there, he found that Hades had already given his wife some pomegranate seeds, hoping that she would thereby stay forever in his keeping. Dismayed at this unexpected down-fall of her hopes, Demeter was about to shut herself up again in the cave, when Zeus, in behalf of the suffering earth, made a compromise with Hades whereby Persephone was to spend half her time with her mother in the land of sunshine and flowers, and the rest with her husband in cold and cheerless Hades. Each spring Hermes was sent to lead Persephone up from the underworld lest her eyes, grown accustomed only to shadows, should be dazzled by the blinding sunlight, and she herself should lose the way. All things awaited her coming; and as soon as her foot touched the winter-saddened earth the flowers bloomed to delight her eyes, the grass sprang up to carpet her way with greenness, the birds sang to cheer her long-depressed spirit, and above her the sun shone brilliantly in the blue Sicilian sky.

Demeter no longer mourned, nor did she again suffer a great famine to afflict the land. The patient old earth smiled again on Persephone's return, for then her mother gave the blighted vegetation a redoubled care. But her happiness did not make the goddess forget the kindly old man who had given her food and shelter at Eleusis, for she returned there and taught the boy Triptolemus all the secrets of agriculture. She also gave him her chariot, and bade him journey everywhere, teaching the people how to plow and sow and reap, and care for their harvests. Triptolemus carried out all her instructions; and as he traveled over the country he was eagerly welcomed alike by prince and peasant until he came to Scythia, where the cruel King Lyncus would have killed him, in a fit of jealous wrath, had not Demeter interfered with timely aid and changed the treacherous monarch into a lynx.

How Apollo Got His Lyre

<u>ᕐᕐᕐᕐᕐᕐᕐᕐᕐ</u>

Hermes was the child of Maia, the eldest of the Pleiades, and lived with his mother in a cave among the mountains. One day, when he was only just big enough to walk, he ran out of doors to play in the sunshine, and saw a spotted tortoise-shell lying in the grass. He laughed with pleasure at sight of the pretty thing, and quickly carried it into the cave. Then he bored holes in the edge of the shell, fastened hollow reeds inside, and with a piece of leather and strings made a lyre of it. This was the first lyre that was ever made, and most wonderful music lay hidden in it.

That night, when his mother was asleep, Hermes crept slyly out of his cradle and went out into the moonlight; he ran to the pastures where Apollo's white cattle were sleeping, and stole fifty of the finest heifers. Then he threw his baby-shoes into the ocean, and bound great limbs of tamarisk to his feet, so that no one would be able to tell who had been walking in the soft sand. After this, he drove the cattle hither and thither in great glee for a while, and then took them down the mountain and shut them into a cave—but one would think from the tracks left in the sand that the cattle had been driven up, instead of down the mountain.

A peasant, who was hoeing in his vineyard by the light of the full moon, saw this wonderful baby pass by, driving the cattle, and could hardly believe his own eyes. No one else saw Hermes; and just at sunrise, the little mischief went home to his mother's cave, slipped in through the keyhole, and in a twinkling was in his cradle with his tortoise-shell lyre held tightly in his arms, looking as if he had been sleeping there all night.

Apollo soon missed his cattle. It happened that the man who had been hoeing his grape-vines by moonlight was still working in the same field. When Apollo asked him whether he had seen any one driving cattle over that road, the man described the baby that he had seen, with the curious shoes, and told him how it had driven the cattle backward and forward, and up and down.

By daylight, the road looked as if the wind had been playing havoc with the young evergreens. Their twigs were scattered here and there, and great branches seemed to have been broken off and blown about in the sand. There were no tracks of any living thing, except the tracks of the cattle, which led in all directions. This was very confusing, but Apollo, knowing that no baby, except his own baby brother, could drive cattle, went straight to Maia's cave.

There lay Hermes in his cradle, fast asleep. When Apollo accused him of stealing his white cattle, he sat up and rubbed his eyes, and said innocently that he did not know what cattle were; he had just heard the word for the first time. But Apollo was angry, and insisted that the baby should go with him to Zeus, to have the dispute settled.

When the two brothers came before Zeus's throne, Hermes kept on saying that he had never seen any cattle and did not know what they were; but as he said so, he gave Zeus such a roguish wink that he made the god laugh heartily. Then he suddenly caught up his lyre, and began to play. The music was so beautiful that all the gods in Olympus held their breath to listen. Even Zeus's fierce eagle nodded his head to the measures. When Hermes stopped playing, Apollo declared that such music was well worth the fifty cattle, and agreed to say no more about the theft. This so pleased Hermes that he gave Apollo the lyre.

Then Apollo, in return for the gift of the wonderful lyre, gave Hermes a golden wand, called the caduceus, which had power over sleep and dreams, and wealth and happiness. At a later time two wings fluttered from the top of this wand, and two golden snakes were twined round it. Besides presenting Hermes with the caduceus, Apollo made him herdsman of the wonderful white cattle. Hermes now drove the fifty heifers back to their pastures. So the quarrel was made up, and the two brothers, Apollo and Hermes, became the best of friends.

On a day when the wind is blowing and driving fleecy white clouds before it, perhaps, if you look up, you will see the white cattle of Apollo. But you will have to look very sharp to see the herdsman, Hermes.

ANGER OF THE GODS

There was rarely something more dangerous in Greek myth than incurring the ire of a god or goddess – unfortunately they were also relatively easy to enrage. While they were subject to all the same emotions as humans, including jealousy and pride, they were also armed with immortality and incredible powers, an ominous combination. Collected here are a selection of stories in which the gods and goddesses punish those who angered them. Observe the fate of those who compared their skills to goddesses such as Athena or Leto in the stories of Arachne and Niobe. Learn the consequences of disrespecting these ancient deities in the unhappy tales of Pentheus and the Rustics. Discover the violent penalty for spying on Artemis as she bathes in the myth of Acteon. And even witness the gods and goddesses turn on one another with the tale of Hebe.

Artemis

Artemis was the goddess of the woods. She was the daughter of Zeus and of the goddess Leto, who had gone through many troubles before Artemis was born. For Zeus had married the beautiful Leto secretly, and when Hera heard of it she was very angry, and drove her away from Mount Olympus. Leto took shelter on the earth, but Hera commanded the earth to deny her rest, and whenever she lay down it began to tremble under her and quaked horribly. She fled like a hunted deer from one end of the world to the other, till after long wanderings she came to the floating island of Delos over which the earth had no power, and here at last she could rest. The island was not fixed to the bottom of the sea, and the waves played roughly with it and tossed it about, so the sea-god Poseidon, who was sorry for Leto, caused four granite pillars to spring up and hold it fast, and ever since that time it has stood perfectly still. Leto had two children, a boy and a girl, and Zeus named them Apollo and Artemis. After the children were born, Hera became kinder, and allowed

Leto to come back to Mount Olympus, and desired the earth to give her rest wherever she wished. The island of Delos was ever afterwards held in great esteem by the Greeks, and they came from long distances in beautifully decked ships to honour the island by offering sacrifices upon it.

Artemis was a glorious goddess, and she chose the woods for her dominion, and the chase for her occupation. She delighted in wandering through the forests with the nymphs who attended her, killing wolves and wild-boars. But she was kind to the tame animals that she met, and stroked and petted them. Her favourite creatures were some beautiful hinds, and she punished anyone who killed them. Artemis towered a head above all her nymphs, and she was also easily to be recognised by her godlike beauty, and by her golden bow and quiver of golden arrows. In the evening she often laid aside her weapons and danced in the moonlight with her maidens; their light footsteps did not even bend the grass, only the next morning, traces of them could be seen in the dew. Often too, when the chase led them past a clear forest lake overshadowed by sweet-smelling trees, they undressed and bathed in the pleasant pool, and the nymphs splashed about in the water and had all kinds of games. Artemis did not marry, for she said she would neither be the wife of a god nor of a man, but would always have her home in the forest among her nymphs.

There was once a hunter named Actaeon, who loved hunting better than anything else, and who honoured Artemis, the goddess of the chase, above all other gods and goddesses. He had fifty splendid hounds who were very fond of their master, and in the morning when he came out of his house they used to crowd round him barking for joy and licking his hands; he had given each of them a special name, and he patted them and talked to them as if they could understand him. They always went out hunting with him, and chased the wild animals which he shot with his arrows. One day Actaeon was out hunting, and it was so hot that about noon he gave his dogs a rest and let them go to sleep, whilst he himself strolled about among the cool bushes looking for a spring where he might quench his thirst. Presently he heard a splashing of water and the laughter of maidens' voices, and going a little nearer, he pushed aside the branch of a tree and beheld the glorious goddess and her nymphs in the bath. He could not turn away his eyes, and for a little while Artemis did not notice him, but when she looked up and saw the hunter who had so forgotten himself, her eyes filled with anger at his having dared to watch her. She raised her beautiful hand, and in a moment Actaeon was changed into a stag with long light feet and branching horns, but still able to think like a man. He shuddered and rushed away to the place where he had left his dogs; they awoke, but they did not know him, and gave chase to him. He tried to make them understand by looking back and calling to them, but no words would come out of his mouth, only a sound like the cry of a stag, and at last they overtook him and tore him to pieces. Thus he was miserably killed by his own dogs, as a punishment for not having turned away his eyes when he came upon the severe goddess at her bath. The dogs wandered for a long time through the forest looking for their master, pining because they could not find him, and refusing to eat. But there was a skilled artist who took pity on them, and he made an image of clay so exactly like Actaeon, that the dogs thought it was their master himself, and were comforted.

Ares, Hephaestus and Hebe

৯৯৯৯৯৯৯৯৯

The three children of Zeus and Hera were Hebe, Ares, and Hephaestus. Hebe, goddess of youth, was cupbearer at the feasts of Olympus and poured from golden flagons the sparkling, ruby-tinted nectar. Many times were the brimming cups emptied and filled again, for the gods loved long draughts of the life-giving nectar that kept off all sickness and decay. No wine of earth's yielding ever appeared at these royal banquets, nor were there seen here the heaped-up platters of food such as mortals crave; for the gods ate only of the divine ambrosia which insured to them eternal youth and beauty.

For so long a time had fair-haired Hebe served at the feasts of Olympus that the gods never thought that she could be deprived of her office; but once, as she was handing Zeus a well-filled cup, she stumbled and fell, and the ruler of gods and men was so angry that he vowed that she should never again be cupbearer. Since no one among the gods was willing to fill this humble position, Zeus was obliged to seek over the earth for some mortal to take the place of poor disgraced Hebe. To make the journey as speedily as possible he assumed the form of an eagle, and spent many days soaring over the land before he found the youth whose slender grace made him feel assured that its possessor would be able to serve the gods less awkwardly than Hebe. On the sunny slopes of Mount Ida he saw a group of youths playing games, and among them was one whom Zeus determined to bear away at once to Olympus. This was Ganymede, a prince of Troy; and the fact that he was no common mortal, but a king's son, did not deter Zeus from swooping down upon the astonished youth, and carrying him aloft on his wings. Whether Ganymede was happy in Olympus we do not know; but the story goes that he remained forever at Zeus's side, and the city of Troy never saw him again, nor did the king his father ever know the reason for his strange disappearance.

Dionysus

Dionysus was the son of Zeus and Semele. Hera, to gratify her resentment against Semele, contrived a plan for her destruction. Assuming the form of Beroë, her aged nurse, she insinuated doubts whether it was indeed Zeus himself who came as a lover. Heaving a sigh, she said, "I hope it will turn out so, but I can't help being afraid. People are not always what they pretend to be. If he is indeed Zeus, make him give some proof of it. Ask him to come arrayed in all his splendors, such as he wears in heaven. That will put the matter beyond a doubt." Semele was persuaded to try the experiment. She asks a favor, without naming what it is. Zeus gives his promise, and confirms it with the irrevocable oath, attesting the river Styx, terrible to the gods themselves. Then she made known her request. The god would have stopped her as she spake, but she was too quick for him. The words escaped, and he could neither unsay his promise nor her request. In deep distress he left her and returned to the upper regions. There he clothed himself in his splendors, not putting on all his

79

terrors, as when he overthrew the giants, but what is known among the gods as his lesser panoply. Arrayed in this, he entered the chamber of Semele. Her mortal frame could not endure the splendors of the immortal radiance. She was consumed to ashes.

Zeus took the infant Dionysus and gave him in charge to the Nysæan nymphs, who nourished his infancy and childhood, and for their care were rewarded by Zeus by being placed, as the Hyades, among the stars. When Dionysus grew up he discovered the culture of the vine and the mode of extracting its precious juice; but Hera struck him with madness, and drove him forth a wanderer through various parts of the earth. In Phrygia the goddess Rhea cured him and taught him her religious rites, and he set out on a progress through Asia, teaching the people the cultivation of the vine. The most famous part of his wanderings is his expedition to India, which is said to have lasted several years. Returning in triumph, he undertook to introduce his worship into Greece, but was opposed by some princes, who dreaded its introduction on account of the disorders and madness it brought with it.

As he approached his native city Thebes, Pentheus the king, who had no respect for the new worship, forbade its rites to be performed. But when it was known that Dionysus was advancing, men and women, but chiefly the latter, young and old, poured forth to meet him and to join his triumphal march.

Mr. Longfellow in his "Drinking Song" thus describes the march of Dionysus (Bacchus in Latin):

"Fauns with youthful Bacchus follow;
Ivy crowns that brow, supernal
As the forehead of Apollo,
And possessing youth eternal.

"Round about him fair Bacchantes,
Bearing cymbals, flutes and thyrses,
Wild from Naxian groves of Zante's
Vineyards, sing delirious verses."

It was in vain Pentheus remonstrated, commanded, and threatened. "Go," said he to his attendants, "seize this vagabond leader of the rout and bring him to me. I will soon make him confess his false claim of heavenly parentage and renounce his counterfeit worship." It was in vain his nearest friends and wisest counsellors remonstrated and begged him not to oppose the god. Their remonstrances only made him more violent.

But now the attendants returned whom he had despatched to seize Dionysus. They had been driven away by the Maenads, but had succeeded in taking one of them prisoner, whom, with his hands tied behind him, they brought before the king. Pentheus, beholding him with wrathful countenance, said, "Fellow! you shall speedily be put to death, that your fate may be a warning to others; but though I grudge the delay of your punishment, speak, tell us who you are, and what are these new rites you presume to celebrate."

The prisoner, unterrified, responded, "My name is Acetes; my country is Mæonia; my parents were poor people, who had no fields or flocks to leave me, but they left me their fishing rods and nets and their fisherman's trade. This I followed for some time, till growing weary of remaining in one place, I learned the pilot's art and how to guide my course by the stars. It happened as I was sailing for Delos we touched at the island of Dia and went ashore. Next morning I sent the men for fresh water, and myself mounted the hill to observe the wind; when my men returned bringing with them a prize, as they thought, a boy of delicate appearance, whom they had found asleep. They judged he was a noble youth, perhaps a king's son, and they might get a liberal ransom for him. I observed his dress, his walk, his face. There was something in them which I felt sure was more than mortal. I said to my men, 'What god there is concealed in that form I know not, but some one there certainly is. Pardon us, gentle deity, for the violence we have done you, and give success to our undertakings.' Dictys, one of my best hands for climbing the mast and coming down by the ropes, and Melanthus, my steersman, and Epopeus, the leader of the sailor's cry, one and all exclaimed, 'Spare your prayers for us.' So blind is the lust of gain! When they proceeded to put him on board I resisted them. 'This ship shall not be profaned by such impiety,' said I. 'I have a greater share in her than any of you.' But Lycabas, a turbulent fellow, seized me by the throat and attempted to throw me overboard, and I scarcely saved myself by clinging to the ropes. The rest approved the deed.

"Then Dionysus (for it was indeed he), as if shaking off his drowsiness, exclaimed, 'What are you doing with me? What is this fighting about? Who brought me here? Where are you going to carry me?' One of them replied, 'Fear nothing; tell us where you wish to go and we will take you there.' 'Naxos is my home,' said Dionysus; 'take me there and you shall be well rewarded.' They promised so to do, and told me to pilot the ship to

Naxos. Naxos lay to the right, and I was trimming the sails to carry us there, when some by signs and others by whispers signified to me their will that I should sail in the opposite direction, and take the boy to Egypt to sell him for a slave. I was confounded and said, 'Let some one else pilot the ship;' withdrawing myself from any further agency in their wickedness. They cursed me, and one of them, exclaiming, 'Don't flatter yourself that we depend on you for our safety,' took my place as pilot, and bore away from Naxos.

"Then the god, pretending that he had just become aware of their treachery, looked out over the sea and said in a voice of weeping, 'Sailors, these are not the shores you promised to take me to; yonder island is not my home. What have I done that you should treat me so? It is small glory you will gain by cheating a poor boy.' I wept to hear him, but the crew laughed at both of us, and sped the vessel fast over the sea. All at once—strange as it may seem, it is true,—the vessel stopped, in the mid sea, as fast as if it was fixed on the ground. The men, astonished, pulled at their oars, and spread more sail, trying to make progress by the aid of both, but all in vain. Ivy twined round the oars and hindered their motion, and clung to the sails, with heavy clusters of berries. A vine, laden with grapes, ran up the mast, and along the sides of the vessel. The sound of flutes was heard and the odor of fragrant wine spread all around. The god himself had a chaplet of vine leaves, and bore in his hand a spear wreathed with ivy. Tigers crouched at his feet, and forms of lynxes and spotted panthers played around him. The men were seized with terror or madness; some leaped overboard; others preparing to do the same beheld their companions in the water undergoing a change, their bodies becoming flattened and ending in a crooked tail. One exclaimed, 'What miracle is this!' and as he spoke his mouth widened, his nostrils expanded, and scales covered all his body. Another, endeavoring to pull the oar, felt his hands shrink up and presently to be no longer hands but fins; another, trying to raise his arms to a rope, found he had no arms, and curving his mutilated body, jumped into the sea. What had been his legs became the two ends of a crescent-shaped tail. The whole crew became dolphins and swam about the ship, now upon the surface, now under it, scattering the spray, and spouting the water from their broad nostrils. Of twenty men I alone was left. Trembling with fear, the god cheered me. 'Fear not,' said he; 'steer towards Naxos.' I obeyed, and when we arrived there, I kindled the altars and celebrated the sacred rites of Dionysus."

Pentheus here exclaimed, "We have wasted time enough on this silly story. Take him away and have him executed without delay." Acetes was led away by the attendants and shut up fast in prison; but while they were getting ready the instruments of execution the prison doors came open of their own accord and the chains fell from his limbs, and when they looked for him he was nowhere to be found.

Pentheus would take no warning, but instead of sending others, determined to go himself to the scene of the solemnities. The mountain Citheron was all alive with worshippers, and the cries of the Maenads resounded on every side. The noise roused the anger of Pentheus as the sound of a trumpet does the fire of a war-horse. He penetrated through the wood and reached an open space where the chief scene of the orgies met his eyes. At the same moment the women saw him; and first among them his own mother, Agave, blinded by the god, cried out, "See there the wild boar, the hugest monster that prowls in these woods! Come on, sisters! I will be the first to strike the wild boar." The whole band rushed upon him, and while he now talks less arrogantly, now excuses himself, and now confesses his crime and implores pardon, they press upon him and wound him. In vain he cries to his aunts to protect him from his mother. Autonoë seized one arm, Ino the other, and between them he was torn to pieces, while his mother shouted, "Victory! Victory! we have done it; the glory is ours!"

So the worship of Dionysus was established in Greece.

There is an allusion to the story of Dionysus and the mariners in Milton's "Comus," at line 46.

"Bacchus that first from out the purple grapes
Crushed the sweet poison of misused wine,
After the Tuscan mariners transformed,
Coasting the Tyrrhene shore as the winds listed
On Circe's island fell (who knows not Circe,
The daughter of the Sun? whose charmed cup
Whoever tasted lost his upright shape,
And downward fell into a grovelling swine)."

Arachne

The hay that so short a time ago was long, lush grass, with fragrant meadow-sweet and gold-eyed marguerites growing amongst it in the green meadow-land by the river, is now dry hay—fragrant still, though dead, and hidden from the sun's warm rays underneath the dark wooden rafters of the barn. Occasionally a cat on a hunting foray comes into the barn to look for mice, or to nestle cosily down into purring slumber. Now and then a hen comes furtively tip-toeing through the open door and makes for itself a secret nest in which to lay the eggs which it subsequently heralds with such loud clucks of proud rejoicing as to completely undo all its previous precautions. Sometimes children come in, pursuing cat or hen, or merely to tumble each other over amongst the soft hay which they leave in chaotic confusion, and when they have gone away, a little more of the sky can be seen through the little window in the roof, and through the wooden bars of the window lower down. Yet, whatever other living creatures may come or go, by those windows of the barn, and high up on its dark rafters, there is always a living creature working, ceaselessly working. When, through the skylight, the sun-god drives a golden sunbeam, and a long shaft of dancing dust-atoms passes from the window to what was once a part of the early summer's glory, the work of the unresting toiler is also to be seen, for the window is hung with shimmering grey tapestries made by Arachne, the spider, and from rafter to rafter her threads are suspended with inimitable skill.

She was a nymph once, they say—the daughter of Idmon the dyer, of Colophon, a city of Lydia. In all Lydia there was none who could weave as wove the beautiful Arachne. To watch her card the wool of the white-fleeced sheep until in her fingers it grew like the soft clouds that hang round the hill tops, was pleasure enough to draw nymphs from the golden river Pactolus and from the vineyards of Tymolus. And when she drove her swift shuttle hither and thither, still it was joy to watch her wondrous skill. Magical was the growth of the web, fine of woof, that her darting fingers span, and yet more magical the exquisite devices that she then wrought upon it. For birds and flowers and butterflies and pictures of all the beautiful things on earth were limned by Arachne, and old tales grew alive again under her creative needle.

To Pallas Athené, goddess of craftsmen, came tidings that at Colophon in Lydia lived a nymph whose skill rivalled that of the goddess herself, and she, ever jealous for her own honour, took on herself the form of a woman bent with age, and, leaning on her staff, joined the little crowd that hung round Arachne as she plied her busy needle. With white arms twined round each other the eager nymphs watched the flowers spring up under her fingers, even as flowers spring from the ground on the coming of Demeter, and Athené was fain to admire, while she marvelled at the magic skill of the fair Arachne.

Gently she spoke to Arachne, and, with the persuasive words of a wise old woman, warned her that she must not let her ambition soar too high. Greater than all skilled craftswomen was the great goddess Athené, and were Arachne, in impious vanity, to dream that one day she might equal her, that were indeed a crime for any god to punish.

Glancing up for a moment from the picture whose perfect colours grew fast under her slim fingers, Arachne fixed scornful eyes on the old woman and gave a merry laugh.

"Didst say *equal* Athené? old mother," she said. "In good sooth thy dwelling must be with the goatherds in the far-off hills and thou art not a dweller in our city. Else hadst thou not spoken to Arachne of *equalling* the work of Athené; *excelling* were the better word."

In anger Pallas Athené made answer.

"Impious one!" she said, "to those who would make themselves higher than the gods must ever come woe unutterable. Take heed what thou sayest for punishment will assuredly be thine."

Laughing still, Arachne made reply:

"I fear not, Athené, nor does my heart shake at the gloomy warning of a foolish old crone." And turning to the nymphs who, half afraid, listened to her daring words, she said: "Fair nymphs who watch me day by day, well do ye know that I make no idle boast. My skill is as great as that of Athené, and greater still it shall be. Let Athené try a contest with me if she dare! Well do I know who will be the victor."

. Then Athené cast off her disguise, and before the frightened nymphs and the bold Arachne stood the radiant goddess with eyes that blazed with anger and insulted pride.

"Lo, Athené is come!" she said, and nymphs and women fell on their knees before her, humbly adoring. Arachne alone was unabashed. Her cheeks showed how fast her heart was beating. From rosy red to white went the colour in them, yet, in firm, low voice she spoke.

"I have spoken truth," she said. "Not woman, nor goddess, can do work such as mine. Ready am I to abide by what I have said, and if I did boast, by my boast I stand. If thou wilt deign, great goddess, to try thy skill against the skill of the dyer's daughter and dost prove the victor, behold me gladly willing to pay the penalty."

The eyes of Athené, the grey-eyed goddess, grew dark as the sea when a thunder-cloud hangs over it and a mighty storm is coming. Not for one moment did she delay, but took her place by the side of Arachne. On the loom they stretched out two webs with a fine warp, and made them fast on the beam.

"The sley separates the warp, the woof is inserted in the middle with sharp shuttles, which the fingers hurry along, and, being drawn within the warp, the teeth notched in the moving sley strike it. Both hasten on, and girding up their garments to their breasts, they move their skilful arms, their eagerness beguiling their fatigue. There both the purple is being woven, which is subjected to the Tyrian brazen vessel, and fine shades of minute difference; just as the rainbow, with its mighty arch, is wont to tint a long tract of sky by means of the rays reflected by

92

the shower; in which, though a thousand different colours are shining, yet the very transition eludes the eyes that look upon it . . . There, too, the pliant gold is mixed with the threads."—OVID.

Their canvases wrought, then did Athené and Arachne hasten to cover them with pictures such as no skilled worker of tapestry has ever since dreamed of accomplishing. Under the fingers of Athené grew up pictures so real and so perfect that the watchers knew not whether the goddess was indeed creating life. And each picture was one that told of the omnipotence of the gods and of the doom that came upon those mortals who had dared in their blasphemous presumption to struggle as equals with the immortal dwellers in Olympus. Arachne glanced up from her web and looked with eyes that glowed with the love of beautiful things at the creations of Athené. Yet, undaunted, her fingers still sped on, and the goddess saw, with brow that grew yet more clouded, how the daughter of Idmon the dyer had chosen for subjects the tales that showed the weaknesses of the gods. One after another the living pictures grew beneath her hand, and the nymphs held their breath in mingled fear and ecstasy at Arachne's godlike skill and most arrogant daring. Between goddess and mortal none could have chosen, for the colour and form and exquisite fancy of the pictures of the daughter of Zeus were equalled, though not excelled, by those of the daughter of the dyer of Colophon.

Darker and yet more dark grew the eyes of Athené as they looked on the magical beauty of the pictures, each one of which was an insult to the gods. What picture had skilful hand ever drawn to compare with that of Europa who,

> "riding on the back of the divine bull, with one hand
> clasped the beast's great horn, and with the other
> caught up her garment's purple fold, lest it might
> trail and be drenched in the hoar sea's infinite spray.
> And her deep robe was blown out in the wind, like
> the sail of a ship, and lightly ever it wafted the
> maiden onward."—MOSCHUS.

Then at last did the storm break, and with her shuttle the enraged goddess smote the web of Arachne, and the fair pictures were rent into motley rags and ribbons. Furiously, too, with her shuttle of boxwood she smote Arachne. Before her rage, the nymphs fled back to their golden river and to the vineyards of Tymolus, and the women of Colophon in blind terror rushed away. And Arachne, shamed to the dust, knew that life for her was no longer worth possessing. She had aspired, in the pride of her splendid genius, to a contest with a god, and knew now that such a contest must ever be vain. A cord hung from the weaver's beam, and swiftly she seized it, knotted it round her white neck, and would have hanged herself. But ere the life had passed out of her, Athené grasped the cord, loosened it, and spoke Arachne's doom:

"Live!" she said, "O guilty and shameless one! For evermore shalt thou live and hang as now, thou and thy descendants, that men may never forget the punishment of the blasphemous one who dared to rival a god."

Even as she spoke, Arachne's fair form dried up and withered. Her straight limbs grew grey and crooked and wiry, and her white arms were no more. And from the beam where the beautiful weaver of Lydia had been suspended, there hung from a fine grey thread the creature from which, to this day, there are but few who do not turn with loathing. Yet still Arachne spins, and still is without a compeer.

"Not anie damzell, which her vaunteth most
In skilfull knitting of soft silken twyne,
Nor anie weaver, which his worke doth boast
In dieper, in damaske, or in lyne,

95

Nor anie skil'd in workmanship embost,
Nor anie skil'd in loupes of fingring fine,
Might in their divers cunning ever dare
With this so curious networke to compare."
—SPENSER.

Thus, perhaps, does Arachne have her compensations, and in days that followed long after the twilight of the gods, did she not gain eternal honour in the heart of every Scot by the tale of how she saved a national hero? Kindly, too, are her labours for men as she slays their mortal enemies, the household flies, and when the peasant—practical, if not favoured by Æsculapius and Hygeia—runs to raid the loom of Arachne in order to staunch the quick-flowing blood from the cut hand of her little child, much more dear to her heart is Arachne the spider than the unknown Athené.

"Also in spinners be tokens of divination, and of knowing what weather shall fall—for oft by weathers that shall fall, some spin or weave higher or lower. Also multitude of spinners is token of much rain."—BARTHOLOMEW.

The sun has not long enough shown his face to dry up the dew in the garden, and behold on the little clipped tree of boxwood, a great marvel! For in and out, and all over its twigs and leaves, Arachne has woven her web, and on the web the dew has dropped a million diamond drops. And, suddenly, all the colours in the sky are mirrored dazzlingly on the grey tapestry of her making. Arachne has come to her own again.

Leto and the Rustics

ʕʕʕʕʕʕʕʕ

Through the tropic nights their sonorous, bell-like booming can be heard coming up from the marshes, and when they are unseen, the song of the bull-frogs would suggest creatures full of solemn dignity. The croak of their lesser brethren is less impressive, yet there is no escape from it on those evenings when the dragon-flies' iridescent wings are folded in sleep, and the birds in the branches are still, when the lilies on the pond have closed their golden hearts, and even the late-feeding trout have ceased to plop and to make eddies in the quiet water. "Krroak! krroak! krroak!" they go—"krroak! krroak! krroak!"

It is unceasing, unending. It goes on like the whirr of the wheels of a great clock that can never run down—a melancholy complaint against the hardships of destiny—a raucous protest against things as they are.

This is the story of the frogs that have helped to point the gibes of Aristophanes, the morals of Æsop, and which have always been, more or less, regarded as the low comedians of the animal world.

Latona, or Leto, was the goddess of dark nights, and upon her the mighty Zeus bestowed the doubtful favour of his errant love. Great was the wrath of Hera, his queen, when she found that she was no longer the dearest wife of her omnipotent lord, and with furious upbraidings she banished her rival to earth. And when Leto had reached the place of her exile she found that the vengeful goddess had sworn that she would place her everlasting ban upon anyone, mortal or immortal, who dared to show any kindness or pity to her whose only fault had been that Zeus loved her. From place to place she wandered, an outcast even among men, until, at length, she came to Lycia.

One evening, as the darkness of which she was goddess had just begun to fall, she reached a green and pleasant valley. The soft, cool grass was a delight to her tired feet, and when she saw the silvery gleam of water she rejoiced, for her throat was parched and her lips dry and she was very weary. By the side of this still pond, where the lilies floated, there grew lithe grey willows and fresh green osiers, and these were being cut by a crowd of chattering rustics.

Humbly, for many a rude word and harsh rebuff had the dictum of Hera brought her during her wanderings, Leto went to the edge of the pond, and, kneeling down, was most thankfully about to drink, when the peasants espied her. Roughly and rudely they told her to begone, nor dare to drink unbidden of the clear water beside which their willows grew. Very pitifully Leto looked up in their churlish faces, and her eyes were as the eyes of a doe that the hunters have pressed very hard.

"Surely, good people," she said, and her voice was sad and low, "water is free to all. Very far have I travelled, and I am aweary almost to death. Only grant that I dip my lips in the water for one deep draught. Of thy pity grant me this boon, for I perish of thirst."

Harsh and coarse were the mocking voices that made answer. Coarser still were the jests that they made. Then one, bolder than his fellows, spurned her kneeling figure with his foot, while another brushed before her and stepping into the pond, defiled its clarity by churning up the mud that lay below with his great splay feet.

Loudly the peasants laughed at this merry jest, and they quickly followed his lead, as brainless sheep will follow the one that scrambles through a gap. Soon they were all joyously stamping and dancing in what had so lately been a pellucid pool. The water-lilies and blue forget-me-nots were trodden down, the fish that had their homes under the mossy stones in terror fled away. Only the mud came up, filthy, defiling, and the rustics laughed in loud and foolish laughter to see the havoc they had wrought.

The goddess Leto rose from her knees. No longer did she seem a mere woman, very weary, hungry and athirst, travelled over far. In their surprised eyes she grew to a stature that was as that of the deathless gods. And her eyes were dark as an angry sea at even.

"Shameless ones!" she said, in a voice as the voice of a storm that sweeps destroyingly over forest and mountain. "Ah! shameless ones! Is it thus that thou wouldst defy one who has dwelt on Olympus? Behold from henceforth shalt thou have thy dwelling in the mud of the green-scummed pools, thy homes in the water that thy flat feet have defiled."

As she spoke, a change, strange and terrible, passed over the forms of the trampling peasants. Their stature shrank. They grew squat and fat. Their hands and feet were webbed, and their grinning mouths became great, sad, gaping openings by which to swallow worms and flies. Green and yellow and brown were their skins, and when they would fain have cried aloud for mercy, from their throats there would come only the *"Krroak! krroak! krroak!"* that we know so well.

And when, that night, the goddess of darkness was wrapped in peace in the black, silver star bespangled robe that none could take from her, there arose from the pond over which the grey willows hung, weeping, the clamour of a great lamentation. Yet no piteous words were there, only the incessant, harsh complaint of the frogs that we hear in the marshes.

From that time the world went well with Leto. Down to the seashore she came, and when she held out her arms in longing appeal to the Ægean islands that lay like purple flowers strewn, far apart, on a soft carpet of limpid blue, Zeus heard her prayer. He asked Poseidon to send a dolphin to carry the woman he loved to the floating island of Delos, and when she had been borne there in safety, he chained the island with chains of adamant to the golden-sanded floor of the sea.

And on this sanctuary there were born to Leto twin children, thereafter to be amongst the most famed of the deathless gods—the god and goddess, Apollo and Artemis.

"...Those hinds that were transformed to frogs
Railed at Leto's twin-born progeny,

Which after held the sun and moon in fee."

—MILTON.

Yet are there times, as we look at the squat, bronze bodies of the frogs—green-bronze, dark brown spotted, and all flecked with gold, the turned-down corners of their wistful mouths, their very exquisite black velvety eyes with golden rims—when the piteous croaks that come forth from their throats of pale daffodil colour do indeed awake a sympathy with their appeal against the inexorable decrees of destiny.

"We did not know! We did not understand! Pity us! Ah, pity us! *Krroak! krroak! krroak!*"

Niobe

The fate of Arachne was noised abroad through all the country, and served as a warning to all presumptuous mortals not to compare themselves with the divinities. But one, and she a matron too, failed to learn the lesson of humility. It was Niobe, the queen of Thebes. She had indeed much to be proud of; but it was not her husband's fame, nor her own beauty, nor their great descent, nor the power of their kingdom that elated her. It was her children; and truly the happiest of mothers would Niobe have been if only she had not claimed to be so. It was on occasion of the annual celebration in honor of Leto and her offspring, Apollo and Artemis,—when the people of Thebes were assembled, their brows crowned with laurel, bearing frankincense to the altars and paying their vows,—that Niobe appeared among the crowd. Her attire was splendid with gold and gems, and her aspect beautiful as the face of an angry woman can be. She stood and surveyed the people with haughty looks. "What folly," said she, "is this!—to prefer beings whom you never saw to those who stand before your eyes! Why should Leto be honored with worship, and none be paid to me? My father was Tantalus, who was received as a guest at the table of the gods; my mother was a goddess. My husband built and rules this city, Thebes, and Phrygia is my paternal inheritance. Wherever I turn my eyes I survey the elements of my power; nor is my form and presence unworthy of a goddess. To all this let me add I have seven sons and seven daughters, and look for sons-in-law and daughters-in-law of pretensions worthy of my alliance. Have I not cause for pride? Will you prefer to me this Leto, the Titan's daughter, with her two children? I have seven times as many. Fortunate indeed am I, and fortunate I shall remain! Will any one deny this? My abundance is my security. I feel myself too strong for Fortune to subdue. She may take from me much; I shall still have much left. Were I to lose some of my children, I should hardly be left as poor as Leto with her two only. Away with you from these solemnities,—put off the laurel from your brows,—have done with this worship!" The people obeyed, and left the sacred services uncompleted.

The goddess was indignant. On the Cynthian mountain top where she dwelt she thus addressed her son and daughter: "My children, I who have been so proud of you both, and have been used to hold myself second to none of the goddesses except Hera alone, begin now to doubt whether I am indeed a goddess. I shall be deprived of my worship altogether unless you protect me." She was proceeding in this strain, but Apollo interrupted her. "Say no more," said he; "speech only delays punishment." So said Artemis also. Darting through the air, veiled in clouds, they alighted on the towers of the city. Spread out before the gates was a broad plain, where the youth of the city pursued their warlike sports. The sons of Niobe were there with the rest,—some mounted on spirited horses richly caparisoned, some driving gay chariots. Ismenos, the first-born, as he guided his foaming steeds, struck with an arrow from above, cried out, "Ah me!" dropped the reins, and fell lifeless. Another, hearing the sound of the bow,— like a boatman who sees the storm gathering and makes all sail for the port,—gave the reins to his horses and attempted to escape. The inevitable arrow overtook him as he fled. Two others, younger boys, just from their tasks, had gone to the playground to have a game of wrestling. As they stood breast to breast, one arrow pierced them both. They uttered a cry together, together cast a parting look around them, and together breathed their last. Alphenor, an elder brother, seeing them fall, hastened to the spot to render assistance, and fell stricken in the act of brotherly duty. One only was left, Ilioneus. He raised his arms to heaven to try whether prayer might not avail. "Spare me, ye gods!" he cried, addressing all, in his ignorance that all needed not his intercessions; and Apollo would have spared him, but the arrow had already left the string, and it was too late.

The terror of the people and grief of the attendants soon made Niobe acquainted with what had taken place. She could hardly think it possible; she was indignant that the gods had dared and amazed that they had been able to do it. Her husband, Amphion, overwhelmed with the blow, destroyed himself. Alas! how different was this Niobe from her who had so lately driven away the people from the sacred rites, and held her stately course through the city, the envy of her friends, now the pity even of her foes! She knelt over the lifeless bodies, and kissed now one, now another of her dead sons. Raising her pallid arms to heaven, "Cruel Leto," said she, "feed full your rage with my anguish! Satiate your hard heart, while I follow to the grave my seven sons. Yet where is your triumph? Bereaved as I am, I am still richer than you, my conqueror." Scarce had she spoken, when the bow sounded and struck terror into all hearts except Niobe's alone. She was brave from excess of grief. The sisters stood in garments of mourning over the biers of their dead brothers. One fell, struck by an arrow, and died on the corpse she was bewailing. Another, attempting to console her mother, suddenly ceased to speak, and sank lifeless to the earth. A third tried to escape by flight, a fourth by concealment, another stood trembling, uncertain what course to take. Six were now dead, and only one remained, whom the mother held clasped in her arms, and covered as it were with her whole body. "Spare me one, and that the youngest! O spare me one of so many!" she cried; and while she spoke, that one fell dead. Desolate she sat, among sons, daughters, husband, all dead, and seemed torpid with grief. The breeze moved not her hair, no color was on her cheek, her eyes glared fixed and immovable, there was no sign of life about her. Her very tongue cleaved to the roof of her mouth, and her veins ceased to convey the tide of life. Her neck bent not, her arms made no gesture, her foot no step. She was changed to stone, within and without. Yet tears continued to flow; and borne on a whirlwind to her native mountain, she still remains, a mass of rock, from which a trickling stream flows, the tribute of her never-ending grief.

The story of Niobe has furnished Byron with a fine illustration of the fallen condition of modern Rome:

"The Niobe of nations! there she stands,
Childless and crownless in her voiceless woe;
An empty urn within her withered hands,
Whose holy dust was scattered long ago;
The Scipios' tomb contains no ashes now:
The very sepulchres lie tenantless
Of their heroic dwellers; dost thou flow,
Old Tiber! through a marble wilderness?
Rise with thy yellow waves, and mantle her distress."

—*CHILDE HAROLD*, IV. 79.

This affecting story has been made the subject of a celebrated statue in the imperial gallery of Florence. It is the principal figure of a group supposed to have been originally arranged in the pediment of a temple. The figure of the mother clasped by the arm of her terrified child is one of the most admired of the ancient statues. It ranks with the Laocoön and the Apollo among the masterpieces of art. The following is a translation of a Greek epigram supposed to relate to this statue:

"To stone the gods have changed her, but in vain;
The sculptor's art has made her breathe again."

Tragic as is the story of Niobe, we cannot forbear to smile at the use Moore has made of it in "Rhymes on the Road":

"'Twas in his carriage the sublime
Sir Richard Blackmore used to rhyme,
And, if the wits don't do him wrong,
'Twixt death and epics passed his time,
Scribbling and killing all day long;
Like Phœbus in his car at ease,
Now warbling forth a lofty song,
Now murdering the young Niobes."

Sir Richard Blackmore was a physician, and at the same time a very prolific and very tasteless poet, whose works are now forgotten, unless when recalled to mind by some wit like Moore for the sake of a joke.

LOVED BY THE GODS

While the dangers of angering a god or goddess might have been clear, it should be noted that inspiring their love came with its own risks. This was particularly true when you were a mortal who captured the attention of such a powerful being. The range of romances between the Greek deities and their earthly counterparts was great, some were doomed from the start, while others had happy endings. None of them could be described as going smoothly, however. Here you will find some of the most iconic love stories from ancient Greek myth, both heartbreaking and inspirational. While Eros and Psyche may be the original fairy-tale partnership, with Psyche overcoming challenge after challenge to be re-united with her husband, many of the relationships recounted here did not end so favourably. Being loved by a god was never easy, and sometimes it was even deadly.

Endymion's Sleep

ᖇᖇᖇᖇᖇᖇᖇᖇᖇ

When the plains below were parched and brown and dusty with the heat of summer, on Mount Latmus all was so still and cool, so fresh and green, that one seemed to be in another world. The mountain was most beautiful of all at night, when the moon drove her chariot overhead, and flooded every tree and all the grassy slopes with her pale light.

Endymion was a young shepherd who led his flocks high up on the sides of this mountain and let them browse on the rich pasturage along the margins of its snow-fed streams. He loved the pure mountain air, and the stillness of the higher slopes, which was broken only by the tinkle of his sheep-bells, or the song of birds. There he dreamed his days away, while his sheep and goats were feeding; or, at night, he leaned his head on a log or a mossy stone and slept with the flock.

Selene, the moon-goddess, loved to visit Mount Latmus; in fact, the mountain belonged, in some sense, to her. It was her influence that made everything there so quiet and beautiful. One night, when she had stolen down from her place in the sky for a walk through one of the flowery meadows of Mount Latmus, she found Endymion there asleep.

The shepherd looked as beautiful as any flower on the mountain, or as the swans which were floating in the lake near by, with their heads tucked under their wings. If it had not been for his regular breathing, Selene would have believed that she stood looking at a marble statue. There, at a little distance, lay his sheep and goats, unguarded, and liable to be attacked by wild beasts. Oh, Endymion was a very careless shepherd! That was the effect of the air on Mount Latmus.

Selene knew that it was the wonderful air of her mountain which had made the shepherd heedless, as well as beautiful, therefore she stayed by his flock all night and watched it herself.

She came the next night and the next, and for many nights, to gaze at the sleeper, and to watch the unguarded flock. One morning, when she returned to the sky, she looked so pale from her watching that Zeus asked her where she had been, and she described the beautiful shepherd she had found on her mountain, and confessed that she had been guarding his sheep.

Then she begged of Zeus that since Endymion was so very, very beautiful he might always look as she had seen him in his sleep, instead of growing old as other mortals must. Zeus answered, "Even the gods cannot give to mortals everlasting youth and beauty without giving them also everlasting sleep; but Endymion shall sleep forever and be forever young."

So there, in a cave, on Mount Latmus, Endymion sleeps on to this day; and his wonderful beauty has not faded in the smallest degree, but is a joy still to all who can climb those lofty heights.

The Death of Adonis

∽∽∽∽∽∽∽∽∽

"The fairest youth that ever maiden's
dream conceived."
Lewis Morris.

The ideally beautiful woman, a subject throughout the centuries for all the greatest powers of sculptor's and painter's art, is Venus, or Aphrodite, goddess of beauty and of love. And he who shares with her an unending supremacy of perfection of form is not one of the gods, her equals, but a mortal lad, who was the son of a king.

As Aphrodite sported one day with Eros, the little god of love, by accident she wounded herself with one of his arrows. And straightway there came into her heart a strange longing and an ache such as the mortal victims of the bow of Eros knew well. While still the ache remained, she heard, in a forest of Cyprus, the baying of hounds and the shouts of those who urged them on in the chase. For her the chase possessed no charms, and she stood aside while the quarry burst through the branches and thick undergrowth of the wood, and the hounds followed in hot pursuit. But she drew her breath sharply, and her eyes opened wide in amazed gladness, when she looked on the perfect beauty of the fleet-footed hunter, who was only a little less swift than the shining spear that sped from his hand with the sureness of a bolt from the hand of Zeus. And she knew that this must be none other than Adonis, son of the king of Paphos, of whose matchless beauty she had heard not only the dwellers on earth, but the Olympians themselves speak in wonder. While gods and men were ready to pay homage to his marvellous loveliness, to Adonis himself it counted for nothing. But in the vigour of his perfect frame he rejoiced; in his fleetness of foot, in the power of that arm that Michael Angelo has modelled, in the quickness and sureness of his aim, for the boy was a mighty hunter with a passion for the chase.

Aphrodite felt that her heart was no longer her own, and knew that the wound that the arrow of Eros had dealt would never heal until she knew that Adonis loved her. No longer was she to be found by the Cytherian shores or in those places once held by her most dear, and the other gods smiled when they beheld her vying with Artemis in the chase and following Adonis as he pursued the roe, the wolf, and the wild boar through the dark forest and up the mountain side. The pride of the goddess of love must often have hung its head. For her love was a thing that Adonis could not understand. He held her "Something better than his dog, a little dearer than his horse," and wondered at her whim to follow his hounds through brake and marsh and lonely forest. His reckless courage was her pride and her torture. Because he was to her so infinitely dear, his path seemed ever bestrewn with dangers. But when she spoke to him with anxious warning and begged him to beware of the fierce beasts that might one day turn on him and bring him death, the boy laughed mockingly and with scorn.

There came at last a day when she asked him what he did on the morrow, and Adonis told her with sparkling eyes that had no heed for her beauty, that he had word of a wild boar, larger, older, more fierce than any he had ever slain, and which, before the chariot of Artemis next passed over the land of Cyprus, would be lying dead with a spear-wound through it.

With terrible foreboding, Aphrodite tried to dissuade him from his venture.

"O, be advised: thou know'st not what it is
With javelin's point a churlish swine to gore,

Whose tushes never sheathed he whetteth still,
Like to a mortal butcher, bent to kill.
[...]
Alas, he naught esteems that face of thine,
To which love's eyes pay tributary gazes;
Nor thy soft hands, sweet lips, and crystal eyne,
Whose full perfection all the world amazes;
But having thee at vantage—wondrous dread!—
Would root these beauties as he roots the mead."

—SHAKESPEARE.

To all her warnings, Adonis would but give smiles. Ill would it become him to slink abashed away before the fierceness of an old monster of the woods, and, laughing in the pride of a whole-hearted boy at a woman's idle fears, he sped homewards with his hounds.

With the gnawing dread of a mortal woman in her soul, Aphrodite spent the next hours. Early she sought the forest that she might again plead with Adonis, and maybe persuade him, for love of her, to give up the perilous chase because she loved him so.

But even as the rosy gates of the Dawn were opening, Adonis had begun his hunt, and from afar off the goddess could hear the baying of his hounds. Yet surely their clamour was not that of hounds in full cry, nor was it the triumphant noise that they so fiercely make as they pull down their vanquished quarry, but rather was it baying, mournful as that of the hounds of Hecate. Swift as a great bird, Aphrodite reached the spot from whence came the sound that made her tremble.

Amidst the trampled brake, where many a hound lay stiff and dead, while others, disembowelled by the tusks of the boar, howled aloud in mortal agony, lay Adonis. As he lay, he "knew the strange, slow chill which, stealing, tells the young that it is death."

And as, *in extremis*, he thought of past things, manhood came to Adonis and he knew something of the meaning of the love of Aphrodite—a love stronger than life, than time, than death itself. His hounds and his spear seemed but playthings now. Only the eternities remained—bright Life, and black-robed Death.

Very still he lay, as though he slept; marble-white, and beautiful as a statue wrought by the hand of a god. But from the cruel wound in the white thigh, ripped open by the boar's profaning tusk, the red blood dripped, in rhythmic flow, crimsoning the green moss under him. With a moan of unutterable anguish, Aphrodite threw herself beside him, and pillowed his dear head in her tender arms. Then, for a little while, life's embers flickered up, his cold lips tried to form themselves into a smile of understanding and held themselves up to hers. And, while they kissed, the soul of Adonis passed away.

"A cruel, cruel wound on his thigh hath Adonis, but a deeper wound in her heart doth Cytherea [Aphrodite] bear. About him his dear hounds are loudly baying, and the nymphs of the wild woods wail him; but Aphrodite with unbound locks through the glades goes wandering—wretched, with hair unbraided, with feet unsandalled, and the thorns as she passes wound her and pluck the blossom of her sacred blood. Shrill she wails as down the woodland she is borne . . . And the rivers bewail the sorrows of Aphrodite, and the wells are weeping Adonis on the mountains. The flowers flush red for anguish, and Cytherea through all the mountain-knees, through every dell doth utter piteous dirge:

'Woe, woe for Cytherea, he hath perished, the lovely Adonis!'"—BION.

Passionately the god besought Zeus to give her back her lost love, and when there was no answer to her prayers, she cried in bitterness: "Yet shall I keep a memorial of Adonis that shall be to all everlasting!" And, as she spoke, her tears and his blood, mingling together, were turned into flowers.

"A tear the Paphian sheds for each blood-drop of Adonis, and tears and blood on the earth are turned to flowers. The blood brings forth the roses, the tears, the wind-flower."

Yet, even then, the grief of Aphrodite knew no abatement. And when Zeus, wearied with her crying, heard her, to his amazement, beg to be allowed to go down to the Shades that she might there endure eternal twilight with the one of her heart, his soul was softened.

"Never can it be that the Queen of Love and of Beauty leaves Olympus and the pleasant earth to tread for evermore the dark Cocytus valley," he said. "Nay, rather shall I permit the beauteous youth of thy love to return for half of each year from the Underworld that thou and he may together know the joy of a love that hath reached fruition."

Thus did it come to pass that when dark winter's gloom was past, Adonis returned to the earth and to the arms of her who loved him.

"But even in death, so strong is love,
I could not wholly die; and year by year,

When the bright springtime comes, and the earth
    lives,
Love opens these dread gates, and calls me forth
Across the gulf. Not here, indeed, she comes,
Being a goddess and in heaven, but smooths
My path to the old earth, where still I know
Once more the sweet lost days, and once again
Blossom on that soft breast, and am again
A youth, and rapt in love; and yet not all
As careless as of yore; but seem to know
The early spring of passion, tamed by time
And suffering, to a calmer, fuller flow,
Less fitful, but more strong."—LEWIS MORRIS.

And when the time of the singing of birds has
come, and the flowers have thrown off their white
snow pall, and the brown earth grows radiant in its
adornments of green blade and of fragrant blossom, we know that Adonis has returned from his
exile, and trace his footprints by the fragile flower
that is his very own, the white flower with the
golden heart, that trembles in the wind as once the
white hands of a grief-stricken goddess shook for
sorrow.

"The flower of Death" is the name that the
Chinese give to the wind-flower—the wood-
anemone. Yet surely the flower that was born of

tears and of blood tells us of a life that is beyond the grave—of a love which is unending.

The cruel tusk of a rough, remorseless winter still yearly slays the "lovely Adonis" and drives him down to the Shades. Yet we know that Spring, with its *Sursum Corda*, will return as long as the earth shall endure; even as the sun must rise each day so long as time shall last, to make

> "Le ciel tout en fleur semble une immense rose
> Qu'un Adonis céleste a teinte de son sang."
> —DE HEREDIA.

Eros and Psyche

♋♋♋♋♋♋♋♋♋

I

In the blue waters of the Ægean Sea, midway between Greece and Egypt, lies the fertile land of Crete. Here, long, long ago, when the gods still walked on earth in human form and the sons of men were as children playing in a fair garden, there ruled a king who was the father of three lovely daughters. They lived in a palace in the rich Omphalian plain, beneath the shade of snow-capped Ida, surrounded by smiling gardens and fruitful vineyards, with a glimpse, away to the southward, of the sparkling Mediterranean Sea. So great was the beauty of these three maidens that their fame went abroad throughout all the land, and wealthy wooers flocked from far and wide to win their hands in marriage. The two elder sisters soon became the brides of two great princes, and were well content to pass their days in the sunshine of their husbands' love and admiration, and to deck themselves with gold and jewels, and listen to the praise of their beauty upon the lips of men. For the gods had given them grace of form and feature, but their souls within were vain and foolish, so that in after-years, when they found their sister more blessed than they, their vanity and envy brought them to an evil end.

The youngest sister, whose name was Psyche, continued to live on at home long after the other two were married. In face and form she was as fair as they, whilst her soul within was so pure and beautiful that it shed a heavenly radiance about her, so that when men looked into her face all thoughts of love and wooing died out of their hearts, and they worshipped her as one of the Immortals. Wherever she passed voices were hushed and heads were bowed in prayer, till at length it was rumoured that Aphrodite herself, the Queen of Love, had come to live with men. The temples stood deserted and the altars bare of sacrifice, and from far and wide men flocked to Psyche with gifts and garlands and songs of praise.

Then foam-born Aphrodite, Queen of Love, was filled with jealousy and wrath that a mortal should usurp her place and name, and she cast about in her mind for some means of revenge.

"Verily, I must make this Cretan maiden rue the day when first men laid my offerings at her feet. I will smite her with so dire a malady that her very beauty shall be turned to scorn, and the heights to

126

which her impious pride hath raised her shall be as nought to the depths of her shame and misery."

Thereupon she sent for her son, the great god Eros, who lords it over gods and men. The poison of his fiery darts none can withstand, and with him it rests to burn men's hearts with the fever of unsatisfied desire, or so to temper the venom of his shafts that it runs like heavenly nectar through the veins. Yet the joy that he gives withal is akin to madness, and the torture of his wrath a frenzy unquenchable.

"Best-beloved son," she said, "if thou carest aught for thy mother's name and fame, thou wilt hasten now to do my bidding. In midmost Crete there dwells a maid—Psyche by name—whose impious pride hath cast dishonour on my godhead. The offerings that are mine by right are cast before her feet. My temples stand devoid of worshippers, who flock to pay her court; and all this not in Crete alone, but from the farthest shores of Hellas men cross the sea in white-winged ships to gaze upon her face. Go now, I pray thee, and smite her with a poisoned arrow from thy bow. Make her to love some loathly monster, deformed in soul and body, and with a passion so shameless and all-consuming that men shall spurn her, even as now they haste to pay their vows. As thou lovest me, go with all speed and do my bidding."

So Eros sped away to fulfil Aphrodite's command, and plant in the heart of Psyche the image of a dark and dreadful monster, and make her love it. As she slept he came and stood beside her, armed with his bow and poisoned arrows. But when he looked upon her his arm fell lifeless by his side, and the arrows slipped out of his hand, for never had he looked on one so fair; and her beauty smote his heart as surely as ever one of his own shafts had pierced a mortal's breast. From that moment he loved her with all his soul, and swore that no harm should ever come to her through him, but that he himself and no other, whether man or monster, should be her bridegroom. And he picked up the arrow and put it back into the sheath.

"If she can trust me," he said, "she shall never feel a wound from one of these. I will carry her away, and she shall be mine; but till the gods are reconciled that I should wed a mortal, and my mother's anger is appeased, I must visit her only in the night-time, and she must not know who I am nor see my face. When the gods have proved her and found her worthy of me, then will I reveal myself to her, and through my love she shall be immortal, and dwell with me for ever in the shining courts of heaven."

And he bent over and kissed her lightly on the lips. She smiled in her sleep and held out her arms towards him, and he knew that his kiss had kindled in her heart the light of love.

Aphrodite, meanwhile, with her mind at rest, took her way along the shell-strewn curve of a sandy bay, and laughing ripples made music at her feet. The Sun was slowly sinking to his bed in Ocean's stream, and Night rode in her crescent car across the calm green vault of heaven. From Aphrodite's feet a broad gold path of light led straight to the sunset realms of Helios, the sun-god, and as she waited on the shore, a band of dolphins ploughed the sea towards her. In their wake came Tritons blowing on soft-voiced conches, and some drew a pearly shell behind and pushed it to the shore and bade her enter.

"Great Helios bids thee to his midnight revelry, O Queen of Love," they cried, "and we are come to guide thee along the golden pathway to the glowing palaces of Sunset Land."

As the goddess stepped into the shell, they blew a loud salute upon their conches, and spread a silken sail above her head, and with music and laughter they crossed the shining sea to the golden halls of Helios.

II

Psyche, meanwhile, all unconscious of the wrath she had kindled in the breast of Aphrodite, was pining away at home in loneliness of heart. Little did she care for the worship that men paid her or for the offerings that they laid at her feet. It was for the love of a husband that she longed, and her soul was starving in the midst of rich gifts and the rapt, adoring gaze of worshippers. Her melancholy fastened on the king her father, and on all the palace, and soothsayers and augurs crowded round the doors with omens, charms, and riddling words, and prophesied all manner of evil.

At last the king could bear it no longer, and he set forth on pilgrimage to Apollo's shrine at Delphi, and made question of the oracle.

"Have the gods ordained that Psyche, my daughter, should die unwed, though the fairest maid on earth, or doth some bridegroom await her who tarrieth long? O god of Light, reveal his name, and save my child from death."

Then the tripod shook, and from the midst of the incense and vapour the priestess made reply,

"Think not of marriage-songs, O king, or bridal torches. On a lonely rock on snow-clad Ida must thou leave thy child, the bride of no mortal man.

But a savage monster shall come, the terror of gods and men, and shall bear her away to his own land, and thine eyes shall see her no more. Wherefore make ready the funeral feast. Bring forth your sable robes of mourning, and bid the minstrels raise a dirge for the dead. For so the gods have willed it."

So the king went sadly home, and his heart was heavy within him. And all the people mourned with him; for they loved the fair princess, with her beautiful sad face and her kind and noble heart. All manner of tales went abroad of the monster she must wed, some saying one thing and some another. But most men thought it must be Talus, the great giant who guarded Crete. Three times every day did he walk round the island, and woe to any stranger who fell in his path or tried to land when he was by. For from top to toe he was made of burning metal—gold and silver and bronze and iron—while through his body ran one single vein that was filled with fire and fastened in his head with a nail. If any man tried to thwart him, he would gather him up in his great bronze arms and hold him to his breast, red-hot with the fire in his vein, and when he was well cooked through he would devour him. Many a long year after, when Jason sailed by with the heroes of the Golden Fleece, Talus rushed down, and would have stopped them from watering their ship, and have turned them adrift on the salt seas to be tortured to death with thirst. But Medea, Jason's dark witch-wife, beguiled him with fair promises, and made him cool his burning body in the sea before she would come near. Then when she had him under her spells she softly drew the nail from his head, and the fire flowed forth from his vein, and all his strength departed, and he died with a curse on his lips for Medea and her wiles. But she only laughed aloud, and bade Jason water the ship and thank the immortal gods that he had a witch-woman to wife. That, however, was long after, and Talus was now in the prime of life, and the terror of all the country-side.

Meanwhile, the land was plunged in mourning, and in the palace all was bustle and confusion in preparation for the funeral rites. All day long the old king sat in his chamber, and looked out towards the lonely heights of Ida, where his daughter was to be left.

"Better that she should die in her maidenhood," he cried, "than wed this terrible monster."

Psyche alone in all the palace was calm, and tried to comfort her father.

"Sire," she said, as she put her arms about his neck, "to look on thy tears is to me more bitter than my fate. Weep not for me, for something within me bids me take comfort, and I hear a sweet voice say, 'Rejoice, beloved, and come with me.' Dark was that day, my father, when first men laid their offerings at my feet, and my heart dwelt apart in its loneliness. And now, if but for one day I may look upon the face of my bridegroom, I would gladly die. For, methinks, it is no monster I must wed."

But the king thought only of the words of the oracle, and would not be comforted.

At length the bridal day dawned, and the sad procession wound slowly from the palace towards Ida. Choruses of singers led the way with solemn dirges for the dead, and the king, uncrowned, followed with his nobles clad in armour and holding blazing torches in their hands. Next came Psyche, all in white, with a bridal veil and garlands, and surrounded by white-robed maidens; and last of all the people of the city followed with loud wailing and lamentation. Up the steep mountain road they went, and the path grew rougher and narrower step by step. On either side the dark rocks frowned down upon them, and echoed to and fro the wailings of the people as they passed, and above them the snow-capped peak of Ida stood out against the summer sky, like a lonely sentinel keeping watch over the plain below. Slowly the shadows of the rocks lengthened across the barren slopes, and the funeral torches shone pale in the glowing sunset light. At last they reached the appointed place beneath the unmelting snow, and on the barren rock they set the maiden, and bade her a sorrowful good-bye. Ever and anon they turned back to look on her as they wound down the mountain-track, and always she waved to them a fond farewell. At length the shadows fell on all the mountain-side, and only the snow-clad peak flashed like a ruby in the last rays of the sun, and as they looked backward for the last time they saw Psyche transformed in the golden light. Her white dress shone like a rainbow, and her golden hair fell about her shoulders like a stream of fire, and as she raised her arm to wave to them she looked like no mortal maid, but a goddess in all her beauty, so that the people hushed their voices and bowed their heads before her. Soon the light faded, and they could see her no more. Sadly they went their way, and all down the mountain-track and across the plain below the torches shone out like pale twinkling stars in the darkness.

Psyche, meanwhile, left alone, pondered sadly on her fate, and wondered what the night would bring. And as she sat and pondered, a soft breeze played about her, filling her veil and robe, and gently she felt herself lifted from the rock and borne through the air, till she was laid down upon a grassy bank sweet with the scent of thyme and violets. Here a deep sleep fell upon her, and she knew no more.

III

Day was dawning when Psyche awoke, and high up in the bright air the larks were singing their morning hymn to the sun, and calling on bird and beast and flower to awake and rejoice in the glad daylight. At first she could remember nothing of what had happened, and wondered where she was; then slowly all the sad ceremony of the day before came back to her—the funeral procession up Mount Ida, the lonely rock on which she had been left, and the soft west wind that had borne her away. So she rose up from the green bank on which she had slept all night, and looked round about her to see what manner of land she was in.

She found herself standing on a hillock in the midst of a fertile plain. Steep cliffs rose up on every side as though to guard the peaceful valley, and keep out any evil thing that would enter in. To the eastward only was there a break in the mountain-chain, and the dale widened out towards the sea.

As Psyche gazed, the golden disc of the sun rose slowly from the water, and his bright rays lit up the grey morning sky and scattered the silvery mist that hung about the treetops. On either side of her was a wood, with a green glade between sloping up towards a marble temple, which flashed like a jewel in the rays of the rising sun. And Psyche was filled with wonder at the sight, for it seemed too fair to be the work of human hands.

"Surely," she thought, "it must be the handiwork of the fire-god Hephaestus, for he buildeth for the immortal gods, who sit on high Olympus, and none can vie with him in craft and skill."

Then she looked about her to see if anyone were near. But all around was quiet and still, with no signs of human habitation. Wondering the more, she drew near to the temple, and went up the marble stairs that led to the entrance. When she reached the top her shadow fell upon the golden gate, and, as she stood doubting what to do, they slowly turned on their hinges, and opened to her of their own accord, and she walked through them into the temple. She found herself in a marble court surrounded by pillars and porticoes which re-echoed the soft music of a fountain in the midst. Through the open doors of the further colonnade she caught a glimpse of cool dark rooms, with carvings of cedar-wood and silver and silken hangings. And now the air was filled with music and sweet voices calling her by name.

"Psyche, lady Psyche, all is thine. Enter in."

So she took courage and entered. All day long she wandered about the enchanted palace discovering fresh wonders at every step. Even before she knew it the mysterious voices seemed to guess every wish of her heart. When she would rest they led her to a soft couch. When she was hungry they placed a table before her spread with every dainty. They led her to the bath, and clothed her in the softest silks, and all the while the air was filled with songs and music.

All this time she had not said a word, for she feared she might drive away the kindly voices that ministered to her. But at last she could keep silence no longer.

"Am I a goddess," she asked, "or is this to be dead? Do those who pass the gates of Death feel no change, nor suffer for what they have done, but have only to wish for a thing to gain their heart's desire?"

The voices gave her never a word in answer, but led her to the chamber where her couch was spread with embroidered coverlets. The walls all round were covered with curious paintings, telling of the deeds of gods and heroes—how golden Aphrodite loved Ares, the god of War, and Apollo the nymph Daphne, whom he changed into a laurel-tree that never fades. There was Ariadne, too, upon her island, whom the young god Dionysus found and comforted in her sore distress; and Adonis, the beautiful shepherd, the fairest of mortal men.

Psyche, tired out by all the wonders she had seen during the day, sank down upon her couch, and was soon asleep. But sleep had not long sealed her lids before she was awakened by a stir in the room. The curtain over her head rustled as though someone were standing beside her. She lay still, almost fainting with terror, scarcely daring to breathe, when she heard a voice softly call her by name.

"Psyche, my own, my beloved, at last I have got thee, my dear one."

And two strong arms were round her and a kiss upon her lips. Then she knew that at last the bridegroom she had waited for so long had come to claim her, and in her happiness she cared not to know who he was, but was content to feel his arms about her and hear her name upon his lips. And so she fell asleep again. When she awoke in the morning her first thought was to look on the face of the husband who had come in the dark night, but nowhere could she find him. All the day she passed in company of the mysterious voices who had ministered to her before; but though their kindness and courtesy was never failing, she wandered disconsolately about the empty halls, longing for the night-time, and wondering whether her lover would come again. As soon as it was dark she went again to her chamber, and there once more he came to her and swore that she was his for evermore, and that nothing should part them. But always he left her before it was light and came to her again when night had fallen, so that she never saw his face nor knew what he was like. Yet so well did she love and trust him that she never cared to ask him his secret. So the days and nights sped swiftly by, for in the daylight Psyche found plenty to amuse her in the enchanted palace and garden, and she did not think of loneliness when every night she could hold sweet converse with her beloved.

But one evening when he came to her he was troubled, and said,

"Psyche, my dear one, great danger threatens us, and I must needs ask thee somewhat that shall grieve thy tender heart."

"Mine own lord," she said, "what can there be that I would not gladly do for thee?"

139

"Well do I know, beloved, that thou wouldst give thy life for me. But that which I ask will grieve thee sore, for thou must refuse the boon thy sisters shall ask thee."

"My sisters! They know not where I am. How, then, can they ask me a boon?"

"Even now they stand upon the lonely rock where thou wast left for me, to see if they can find thee or learn aught of thy fate. And they will call thee by name through the echoing rocks, but thou must answer them never a word."

"What, my lord! wouldst thou have my sisters go home disconsolate, thinking that I am dead? Nay, surely, thou wouldst not be so hard of heart? But let me bid the soft west wind, that wafted me hither, bring them too, that they may look upon my happiness and take back the tidings to mine aged sire."

"Psyche, thou knowest not what thou askest. Foolish of heart are thy sisters, and they love the trappings and outward show of woe, and with their mourning they wring their father's aching heart till he can bear it no more. So he hath sent them forth to see whether they can hear aught of thy fate. And, full of their own hearts' shallow grief, they seek thee on the mountain-side, thinking to find thy bones bleaching in the rays of the sun. Were they to see thy happiness, their hearts would be filled with envy and malice. They would speak evil of me, and taunt thee on thine unknown lord, and bid thee look upon my face and see lest I be some foul monster. And Psyche, mine own wife, the night that thou seest my face shall be the night that shall part us for evermore, and thy first look shall be thy last. Therefore answer them not, I pray thee, but stay with me and be my bride."

And Psyche was troubled at these words, for she thought her husband wronged her sisters. Nevertheless, unwilling to displease him, she said,

"I will do thy will, my lord, even as thou sayest."

Yet all the day long she thought on her sisters wandering on the bleak mountain-side, and how they would call for her by name, and at length go sadly home to her father's house and bring no comfort. The more she thought on it the sadder she became, and when her husband came to her, her face was wet with tears. In vain he tried to comfort her. She only sobbed the more.

"All my joy is turned to bitterness," she said, "when I think on the grief that bows down my father's heart. If but for one day I could bring my sisters here and show them my happiness, they would bear the news to him, and in my joy he would be happy too. Let them but come and look at this fair home of mine, and surely it will not harm me or thee, my dear lord?"

"I have not the heart to refuse thee, Psyche," he said, "though it goeth against me to grant this. I fear that evil will come. If they ask thee of me, answer them not."

Psyche was overjoyed at his consent, and thanked him, and put her arms about his neck and said,

"My dearest lord, all thou sayest I will do. For wert thou Eros, the god of Love himself, I could not love thee more."

IV

The next day, when Psyche was left alone, she went out into the valley to see whether she could hear her sisters calling her. And sure enough, she had not gone far, when high up above her head, from the top of the cliff, she heard her name, "Psyche, O Psyche! where art thou?" At this she was overjoyed,

"O gentle Zephyr!" she called, "O fair west wind! waft, oh, waft my sisters to me!"

Scarcely had she said the words than she saw her sisters gently borne down from the cliff above and set upon the ground beside her. She fell upon their necks and kissed them.

142

"Ah, my dear sisters," she cried, "how happy am I to see you! Welcome to my new home. See, I am not tortured, as you thought. Nay, my life is bliss, as you shall see for yourselves. Come, enter in with me."

And she took them by the hand and led them through the golden gates. The ministering voices played soft music in the air, and a rich feast was spread before them. All through the palace Psyche led them, and showed them all her treasures, and brought out her choicest jewels, and bade them choose out and keep as many as they wished.

All this time, though there was no corner of the palace that she kept hidden from them, she spoke no word of her mysterious husband. At length they could contain their curiosity no longer, and one made bold to ask her,

"Psyche, thou livest not here alone, of a surety. Yet where is thy lord? All thy treasures hast thou shown us, but him, the giver of all, we have not seen. Who is he, then? Surely he, whom the winds and bodiless voices obey, must be a god, and no mortal man. Tell us of him, we pray thee."

And Psyche remembered her husband's warning.

"My lord," she said, "is a huntsman bold, and over hill and dale he rides this day after the swift-footed stag. As fair as the dawn is he, and the first down of youth is on his cheek. All through the hours of sunlight he goeth forth to the chase, and at eventime he returneth to me."

It was now close on night, and the shadows fell long across the cool green lawns of the garden. Psyche bethought her that it was high time for her sisters to go, before they could ply her with questions. So, kissing them farewell, and sending many a loving message to the king her father, she called on Zephyr to waft them away to the top of the cliff.

Hitherto the surprise and wonder at all they had seen and heard had filled the minds of the two sisters. But when they found themselves once more alone upon the barren mountain-slopes, they had leisure to think and compare their lot with that of their sister. Before they had seen her golden halls they had been quite content with their own palaces. But these now seemed humble beside the splendours they had just left. Their shallow hearts were quite filled up with the image of themselves, and they had no room left for their sister. But now her good fortune forced the remembrance of her upon them, and they were filled with an envy and jealousy of her which conquered even their love for themselves. They could not be content to return once more to their homes, and receive the homage of their husbands and their households. Their one thought was how they might spoil her happiness. For the hatred that is born of self-love is an all-consuming passion that burns up every kind and noble thought, as a forest fire burns up the tall trees that stand in the path of its fury.

"How cruel and unjust," cried one, "that she, the youngest, should be blest so far above us both. My lord is a very beggar to him who giveth Psyche her golden halls to dwell in."

"Yea, and mine is an old man by the side of this beardless youth. Sister, thy grief and mine are one. Side by side let us work, and verily her cunning shall be great if she can avail against us and keep her ill-gotten wealth."

"Thou sayest well. 'Twas from pride that she welcomed us to her halls to flaunt her riches before us. Sister, I am with thee. Quickly let us plan some plot to unrobe this upstart maiden of her vaunted godhead."

Whereupon they agreed together to bring their father no word of Psyche's happiness. They tore their robes and loosed their hair, as though all this while they had been wandering over the rough mountain rocks.

"Ah, sire," they cried, "how can we tell thee the evil tidings? Nowhere can we find our sister, or any trace of her. Verily, the oracle lieth not, and she is the bride of some fell monster."

Their cruel words smote their father to the heart, and quenched the feeble spark of hope that still burned in his breast. And when all hope leaves the heart of man, life leaves him, too. So the old king died, and his blood was on the hands of his own children, and one day they paid the penalty with their lives.

Meanwhile, Psyche lived on in the happy valley in blissful content. Her husband would often warn her that her sisters were plotting her ruin, but she would listen to nothing against them. At last one night he said,

"Psyche, to-morrow thy sisters will seek thee once again. This time they will not wait for Zephyr to bear them down, but, trusting themselves to the barren air, they will hurl themselves from the cliff, and be dashed to pieces on the rocks below. Leave them to their fate. 'Twill be due penalty for their crime, and 'tis the only way that we can be saved, beloved."

"My lord," cried Psyche, "thy cruelty would kill my love for thee, were it not immortal. But, in very truth, all my joy would be slain did I know that my sisters were killed when I could have saved them. Oh, dearest husband, by the love that makes us one, I beseech thee, send Zephyr once more to bear my sisters hither."

And she sobbed so pitifully and prayed so earnestly that once again he had not the heart to refuse.

So about noontide the next day Psyche heard loud knocking and cries at the door, and she hastened to open it herself to her sisters. Again she kissed them, and bade them welcome, and they deceived her with flattery and honeyed words, and when she was off her guard one said,

"Come, tell us, Psyche, thy husband's name. Among the immortal gods, where doth he take his place, and why is he not here to greet us?"

"My husband," she replied, "is a rich merchant. Many a long year hath it taken to build up all the fortune you behold, for already the hair about his temples is touched with snow. And this day hath he gone a long journey to a distant town in search of rich merchandise, and he returneth not till the setting of the sun."

Then quickly she called on Zephyr to bear them away before they could ply her with questions.

When her husband came that night he was more troubled than before, and begged her to see them no more, but let them be dashed to death on the rocks if they troubled her again.

147

Her pure heart, however, would believe no evil of them; and in this one thing she disobeyed her lord.

V

Meanwhile, the second visit of the sisters to Psyche in her beautiful home had but served to add fuel to the fire of their envy. When they remembered her confusion and the different tales she had told them about her unknown lord, jealousy whispered in their ears that all her happiness depended on the keeping of her secret, and that secret they straightway determined to know.

"'Tis a strange lord, methinks," said one, "who in the waxing and waning of a single moon doth change from a beardless boy to a grave and reverend merchant whose hair is touched with snow."

"True, sister. And therein lieth the secret of her happiness. Her lying tale but proves that she hath never seen her lord. And verily, he who would hide his face from the queen of his heart must be some child of the Immortals, whose love for an earth-born maid must be hid from gods and men."

"Yea, and they who are loved of the Immortals are themselves immortal, too, and their seed after them. Truly, sister, that Psyche should be a goddess is more than I can bear."

"I feel with thee! It is not meet that the youngest should have all. Let us invent some lying tale which shall make her look upon her lord, and break the spell which binds him to her."

"What sayest thou to the words of the oracle that doomed her to wed a monster? Let us go to her and say that now we know this to be true, and beg her to flee from a fate so vile."

So once more they trusted themselves to Zephyr, for Psyche had prevailed upon her lord to promise that, so long as her sisters should do her no harm, Zephyr should always be waiting to carry them to and fro from her.

Early the next day she was aroused from sleep by the sound of weeping and lamentation at her door, and she hastened to meet her sisters, fearing some ill news. And they fell upon her neck, crying,

"Alas, alas, for thine evil fate!"

"Mine evil fate, sisters? What mean ye? All is well with me."

"Ah, so thou thinkest in thine heart's innocence. Even so falleth the dove a victim to the hawk that wheeleth above."

"What talk is this of doves and hawks? Come, my sisters, weep no more, for in this pleasant vale even the winds of heaven breathe gently on me, so good and great is my lord who commandeth them."

"Thy lord! Hast ever seen his face, child, that thou callest him good and great?"

"Nay," she answered, blushing to think that they had guessed her secret, "'tis true I have not seen his face, but what need to look upon him when all around me breathes of his love for me?"

"Hast never heard tell of foul monsters that wed with the daughters of men, and come to them only in the night season, when the darkness can hide their deformity? They cast a spell about their victims, and by their wiles and enchantments they make all things about them seem fair. But one day, when they have had their fill, and tire of the maid they have won, lo! at a word the pleasant palaces and gardens vanish into air, and she is left all ashamed and deserted, and scorned by gods and men. Ah, sister, be warned by those who wish thee well, and flee from thy vile lot ere all is lost. Even yesterday, when we left thee, we saw a monstrous shape that glided after us through the wood, and we fled in terror, knowing it was thy lord, who would not have us near thee. Come with us now, and be saved."

When Psyche heard their words she was very troubled. Truly, 'twas strange that her lord should be loath for her to see her sisters, unless, indeed, it was even as they said, and she was the prey of some terrible beast. Yet his kind and loving words and his tender thought for her welfare and all the beauty that surrounded her gave the lie to such a thought.

"My dear sisters," she cried, "I thank you for your loving fears for me, but it cannot be as you say. Though I have never looked upon my lord, these fair halls and gardens do but mirror forth the beauty of his soul, and I know that he is true."

"Then why doth he hide his face? At least, if thou wilt not flee with us now, do but put him to the test when he comes this night. A glimpse at his form will tell thee that our tale is true; and if by some strange chance it be not so, what harm can one glance do?"

Thus they tempted her, and made her doubt her lord, though sore against her will. So it often happens that the pure of heart are tortured by the doubts which the wicked plant in their breasts. As little does a young bird in the greenwood suspect the hunter's snare as did Psyche in her loving innocence suspect the malicious envy of her sisters.

But they were filled with joy at the success of their plot, and when Zephyr had borne them to the top of the cliff they could contain their gladness no longer, but fell upon each other's necks and kissed and danced for glee.

But Psyche at their bidding made ready to look

151

upon her lord that night. Under a chair she placed a lighted lamp in readiness, and shrouded it about, that the light might not shine into the room and betray her purpose. Trembling she went to bed that night, for she hated the deed she must do. At the usual hour her lord came and spoke lovingly to her, and kissed her, but her words died away upon her lips, and she shuddered at his embrace. In time he fell asleep, and his breathing was gentle and even as that of a child sweetly dreaming in its innocence of heart. Then she rose up silently in the dead of night, and walking softly to the chair, she took the lamp from beneath and turned on tiptoe to the bed. High above her head she held the light, that the rays might fall more gently on him as he slept, and with bated breath she drew near and looked on him. As she looked, the blood rushed headlong through her veins, and her heart beat fast within her, and her limbs seemed turned to water as she bent forward to look more closely. For on the bed, wrapped in deep slumber, lay no terrible monster, as she feared, but the youngest and fairest of the Immortals—Eros, the great god of Love. The gleam of his golden locks was as sunshine on the summer sea, and his limbs like the eddying foam. From his shoulders sprang two mighty wings bright as the rainbow, and by his side lay his quiver and darts. As he moved restlessly in the light of the lamp she heard her name upon his lips. With a low cry she fell on her knees beside him, and as she did so her arm grazed the point of an arrow placed heedlessly in the sheath. The poison ran like liquid fire through her veins, and set her heart aflame, and with blazing cheeks she bent over and kissed him on the lips. As she did so the lamp trembled in her hand, and a drop of the burning oil fell upon his shoulder, and he started up and found her bending over him.

"Ah, wretched, wretched Psyche!" he cried; "what hast thou done? Couldst thou not trust me, who gave thee all the happiness thou hast ever known?"

"My lord, my lord, forgive me! I would but prove to my sisters by mine own eyes' witness that thou wert not the monster that they dreaded."

"Thrice foolish maid! Knowest thou not that doubt driveth away love? Did I not tell thee that thy first look would be thy last? From a terrible fate I saved thee when Aphrodite bade me strike thee with my shaft and make thee love some terrible beast. When I went forth to do her bidding thy grace and beauty conquered me, and I took thee away to be my bride; and in time, hadst thou proved worthy, my mother and all the great gods that rule above would have forgiven me, and shed on thee the gift of immortality, to live with me for ever in the courts of heaven. But now all is lost, and I must leave thee."

"Ah, my lord, great is my sin, but I love thee, and my soul is thine. Over the whole wide world would I wander, or be slave to the meanest of men, so be it I could find thee again. Ah, dearest lord! tell me not that all hope is gone."

One moment he was silent, as though doubting her. Then he answered,

"One way there lieth before thee, if thy courage prove greater than thy faith—one only way, by which thou canst reach me—the long rough path of trial and sorrow. Heaven and earth shall turn against thee; for men win not immortality for a sigh. Yet will I help thee all I may. In thine own strength alone thou wouldst faint and die by the way, but for every step thou takest I will give thee strength for two. And now farewell! I can tell thee no more, neither linger beside thee. Fare thee well, fare thee well."

As he vanished from her eyes Psyche fell senseless on the floor, and for many a long hour she lay there, hearing and seeing nothing, as though life itself had fled.

VI

Meanwhile the two sisters were waiting in a frenzy of impatience to know whether success had crowned their evil plot. If the doubt they had planted in Psyche's breast had borne fruit, and she had dared to disobey her lord, they knew full well that all her happiness would have vanished like a dream. Yet, fearing the anger of him whom the winds of heaven obeyed, they dared not trust themselves to Zephyr, who had carried them down before. So they wandered restlessly from room to room, and peered from the windows, hoping that Psyche in her misery would come to them and beg for succour in her evil plight. There was nothing they would have loved better than to spurn her from their doors and taunt her on the retribution which had fallen on her vanity. But all day long they waited, and yet she came not, so that at length they parted and went each one to her couch.

But the night was hot and sultry, and the eldest sister lay on her bed and tossed restlessly from side to side, and could not sleep. At length she went to the casement and drew aside the curtain and looked out on the starry night, and when she had cooled her burning brow she went back to her couch. Just as she was about to fall asleep she felt a shadow pass between her and the light from the window, and she opened her eyes, and her heart beat fast; for straight in the path of the moonbeams stood Eros, the great god of Love, and his wings stood out black against the starlit sky as he leant on his golden bow. Though his face was dark in the shadow, his eyes seemed to pierce through to her heart as she lay still and trembling with fear. But he spoke softly to her with false, honeyed words.

"Lady, thy sister Psyche, whom I chose out from the daughters of men, hath proved false and untrue, and lo! now I turn my love to thee. Come thou in her stead and be mistress in my palace halls, and I will give thee immortality. Lo! even now Zephyr awaits thee on the mountain-top to bear thee away to my home."

So saying, he faded from her sight. Her wicked heart was filled with joy when she heard of Psyche's fall, and she rose up in the dead of night and put on her gayest robe and brightest gems. Without so much as a look on the prince her husband she went out to the mountain-top. There she stood alone, and called softly to Zephyr,

"O Zephyr, O Zephyr, O fair west wind, waft me, oh waft me away to my love!"

Without waiting she threw herself boldly down. But the air gave way beneath her, and with a terrible cry she fell faster and faster, down, down, to the gulf below, and was dashed to pieces on the rocks; and from the four quarters of heaven the vultures gathered and fed upon her flesh.

As for the second sister, to her, too, the god appeared and spoke false honeyed words, and she too went forth alone; and in the morning her bones lay gleaming white beside her sister's on the rocks below.

VII

When Psyche awoke from her swoon, she looked around her in bewilderment, for the scene which met her eyes was the same, and yet so different. The forest-trees waved their arms gently in the breeze, and whispered to each other in the glad morning light, and in the hedges the birds sang sweet songs of joy; for the skies were blue, and the grass was green, and summer was over the land. But Psyche sat up with a dull grief in her heart, feeling over her the dim shadow of a half-forgotten woe that meets those who awake from sleep. At first she wondered where she was, for her clothes were wet with dew, and looking round the still familiar scene, she saw the green glade in the forest, but no shining palace at the top. Then like a flash she remembered the night, and how by her doubt she had forfeited all her happiness, and she lay on the ground and sobbed and prayed that she might die. But soon tired out with weeping, she grew calmer, and remembered the words of her lord—how she could find him again only after long wandering and trial. Though her knees gave way beneath her, and her heart sank at the thought of setting out alone into the cruel world, she determined to begin her search forthwith. Through the dark forest she went, and the sun hid his face behind the pine-tops, and great oaks threw shadows across her path, in weird fantastic forms, like wild arms thrust out to seize her as she passed. With hurrying steps and beating heart she went on her way till she came out on the bleak mountain-side, where the stones cut her tender feet and the brambles tore her without mercy. But on and on she struggled along the stony road, till the path grew soft beneath her, and sloped gently downwards to the plain. Here through green fields and smiling pastures a river wound slowly towards the sea, and beyond the further bank she saw the smoke from the homesteads rise blue against the evening sky. She quickened her steps, for already the shadows from the trees fell long across the fields, and the grass turned to gold in the light of the dying day. And still between her and shelter for the night lay many a broad meadow and the silver stream to cross. As she drew nearer she looked this way and that for a ford, but seeing none, she gathered together her courage, and breathing a prayer to the gods, stepped into the water. But she was weak and faint with fasting, and at every step the water grew deeper and colder, and her strength more feeble, till at length she was borne off her feet, and swept away by the hurrying tide. In her agony she cried out,

"O god of Love, have mercy and save me ere I die, that I may come to thee!"

Just as she was about to sink, she felt a strong arm seize her and draw her up on the opposite shore. For a while she lay faint and gasping for breath; but as her strength returned, she heard close beside her soft notes of music, and she opened her eyes to see whence the sweet sounds came. She found herself lying beneath a willow-tree, against which leant a strange musician. For his head and shoulders and arms were those of a man, but his legs and feet were thin and hoofed, and he had horns and a tail like a goat. His ears were pointed, his nose was wide and flat, and his hair fell unkempt and wild about his face. Round his body he wore a leopard's skin, and he made sweet music on a pipe of reeds. At first she was terrified at the sight of this strange creature, but when he saw her look up at him, he stopped playing, and smiled at her; and when he smiled he puckered his face in a thousand wrinkles, and his eyes twinkled merrily through his wild elf-locks, so that none could look on him and be sad. In spite of all her woes Psyche fairly laughed aloud as he began to caper round her on his spindle legs, playing a wild dance-tune the while. Faster and faster he went, and up and down, and round and round, till, with a last shrill note on his pipe and a mad caper in the air, he flung himself on the grass beside her.

"Have I warmed the blood back to thy heart, fair maid?" he asked, "or shall I dance again the mad dance that drives away cold and despair?"

"Nay, merry monster, even now my sides ache with laughter. But tell me, who art thou, that savest damsels in distress, and drivest away their sorrow with thy wild piping and dance?"

"I am the god of the forest and woodland and broad wide pasture lands. To me the shepherd prays to give increase to his flocks, and the huntsman for a good day's sport. In the evening, when the moon shines high o'erhead, and the sky is bright with stars, I take my pipe and play my lays in the dim dark forest glades. To the sound of my music the brook murmurs sweetly, the leaves whisper softly o'erhead, the nymphs and naiads forget their shyness, and the hamadryad slips out from her tree. Then the eyes of the simple are opened, and on the cool, green by the side of the silver stream the goatherd, the neatherd and the young shepherd-lad dance hand-in-hand with the nymphs, and the poet, looking forth from his window, cries, 'How sweet are the pipes of Pan!'

"But when the dark storm-cloud rides over the sky, and the streams rush swollen with rain, with fleet foot I hurry through woodland and dell, and over the bleak mountain-tops; the crash of my hoofs on the rocks sounds like thunder in the ears of men, and the shriek of my pipe like the squall of the wild storm-wind. And I rush through the midst of the battle when the trumpets are calling to arms; but above the blare of the bugle men hear the shrill cry of my pipes. Then the archer throws down his bow, and the arm of the spearman falls limp, and their hearts grow faint with panic at the sound of the pipes of Pan. Nay, turn not from me in terror, lady," he added, as Psyche made as though she would flee, "for I wish thee no ill. 'Tis gods mightier than I who have made me goat-footed, with the horns and the tail of a beast. But my heart is kindly withal, or I would not have saved thee from the stream."

Once more he smiled his genial smile, and

puckered his face like the ripples on a lake when a breeze passes over,

"Come, tell me who art thou, and how can I help thee?"

Then Psyche told her tale, and when she had finished Pan was silent for a time, as though lost in thought. At length he looked up, and said,

"Thou seekest the great god Eros? I would that I could help thee, lady; but love once fled is hard to find again. Easier is it to win the dead to life than to bring back love that doubt hath put to flight. I cannot help thee, for I know not how thou canst find him, or where thou must seek. But, if thou wilt journey further, and cross many a long mile of pasture and woodland, thou wilt come to the rich corn-lands and the shrine of Demeter, the great Earth Mother. She knows the secret of the growing corn, and how the rich fruits ripen in their season, and she will have pity on a maid like thee, because of her child Persephone, whom Hades snatched away from her flowery meadows and dragged below to be Queen of the Dead. Three months she lives with him, the bride of Death, in the dark world of shades, and all the earth mourns for her. The trees shed their leaves like tears on her grave, and through their bare branches the wind sings a dirge. But in the spring-time she returns to her mother, and the earth at her coming puts on her gayest robe, and the birds sing their brightest to welcome her back. At her kiss the almond-tree blushes into bloom, and the brook babbles merrily over the stones, and the primrose and violet and dancing daffodil spring up wherever her feet have touched. Go, then, to Demeter's shrine; for if thy love is to be sought on earth, she will tell thee where to go; but if to find him thou must cross the dark river of death, her child Persephone will receive thee."

He then pointed out to her the path to the village, where she could get shelter for the night, and Psyche, thanking him, went on her way, gladdened at heart by the genial smile of the wild woodland god.

That night she slept in a shepherd's cottage, and in the morning the children went out with her to point out the road she must go. The shepherd's wife, standing at the door, waved to her with her eyes full of tears. She had maidens of her own, and she pitied the delicate wanderer, for Psyche's beautiful face had shed a light in the rude shepherd's hut which the inmates would never forget.

VIII

So Psyche went on her journey, often weak and fainting for food, and rough men laughed at her torn clothes and bleeding feet. But she did not heed their jeers and insults, and often those who had laughed the loudest when she was a little way off, were the first to hush their rude companions when they saw her near. For her face was fairer than the dawn and purer than the evening star, so that the wicked man turned away from his sin when he saw it, and the heart of the watcher was comforted as he sat by the sick man's bed.

At length, as Pan had told her, she came to the rich corn-lands where Demeter has her shrine. Already the valleys were standing thick with corn, for it was close on harvest-time, and on the hillsides the purple grapes hung in heavy clusters beneath the tall elm-branches. As she drew near the temple, a band of harvesters came out. They had just placed the first-fruits of the corn in the shrine, and now they were trooping to the fields, a merry throng of young men and maidens. Psyche stood back shyly as they passed, but they heeded her not, or at most cast a curious glance at her ragged clothes and bruised feet. When they had passed her, and she had heard their merry laughter and chatter die away down the lane, she ventured to enter the temple. Within all was dark and peaceful. Before the altar lay sheaves of corn and rich purple clusters of grapes, whilst the floor was strewn with the seeds and bruised fruits which the harvesters had let fall when they carried in their offerings. Hidden in a dark corner Psyche found the temple-sweeper's broom, and, taking it, she swept up the floor of the temple. Then, turning to the altar steps, she stretched forth her hands and prayed,

"O Demeter, great Earth Mother, giver of the golden harvest—O thou who swellest the green corn in the ear, and fillest the purple vine with gladdening juice, have mercy on one who has sinned. For the sake of thy child, Persephone, the Maiden, have pity on me, and tell me where in the wide world I can find Eros, my lord, or whether to the dark land I must go to search for him."

So she prayed, and waited for an answer; but all was still and dark in the temple, and at length she turned sorrowfully away, and leant her head against a pillar and wept. And, because she had walked many a long mile that day, and had not eaten since dawn, she sank down exhausted on the ground, and gradually her sobs grew fewer and fainter, and she fell asleep.

As she slept she dreamt the temple was dark no more, but into every corner shone a soft clear light, and looking round to see whence it came, she saw, on the altar steps, the form of a woman, but taller and grander than any woman of earth. Her robe of brown gold fell in stately folds to her feet, and on her head was a wreath of scarlet poppies. Her hair lay in thick plaits on her bosom, like ripe corn in the harvest, and she leant on a large two-handed scythe. With great mild eyes she looked at Psyche as one who has known grief and the loss of loved ones, and can read the sorrows of men's hearts.

"Psyche," she said, "I have heard thy prayer, and I know thy grief, for I, too, have wandered over the earth to find the child of my love. And thou must likewise wander and bear to the full the burden of thy sin; for so the gods have willed it. This much can I tell thee, and no more. Thou must go yet further from the land of thy birth, and cross many a rough mountain and foaming torrent, and never let thy heart grow faint till thou come to a temple of Hera, the wife of Zeus the All-seeing. And if she find thee worthy, she will tell thee how thou must seek thy love."

So saying, she faded from her sight, and Psyche awoke and found the temple cold and dark. But in her heart she cherished the image of the great Earth Mother, with her large eyes full of pity, and set out comforted on her journey.

Too long would it be to tell of all her wanderings and all the hardships of the road, but many a moon had waxed and waned before she stood on the brow of a hill looking down on Hera's shining temple. Down the hill she went, and up the marble steps, and men stood aside as she passed, for her face was fairer than before, and she no longer shrank back like a hunted thing, but walked with the swinging gait of those whose feet the kind earth has hardened, and the breezes of heaven have fanned the fire in their eyes. In her heart she knew that she had conquered and borne the terrors of the path with no coward's fears, and she prayed that Hera might find her worthy of doing great deeds to win back her lord. Then she stood before the altar, and made her prayer,

"O Hera, golden-throned, who sittest on the right hand of Zeus—O thou who, when the marriage-torch is lit, doth lead the bride and bridegroom to their home, and pourest blessings on their wedded love, have mercy on me, and show me where I may find my lord. Far have I wandered, and drunk deep of sorrow's cup, but my heart is strong for any task that shall win back my love to me."

Thus she prayed, and bowed her head before the great white statue of the goddess. Even as she spoke, the statue seemed to change and rise from the ivory throne in the shape of a woman tall and exceeding fair. Her robes were like the clouds at sunset, and her veil like the mountain mist; on her head she wore a crown of gold, and the lightning played about her feet as she gazed at Psyche with eyes that pierced through to her soul.

"Psyche," she said, "I have heard thy prayer, and I know that thou art true. For I am the wife of Zeus, who seeth all things, and he hideth naught from me. Well I know that thou hast wandered far, and suffered at the hands of men. But greater trials await thee yet, before thou canst find thy lord. Thou must be slave to foam-born Aphrodite, the pitiless goddess of Love. And she will try thee sorely, and put thee to many a hard test ere she will forgive thee and think thee worthy of her son Eros, or of the godhead men gave thee long ago. But if thou overcomest her wrath, thou hast overcome death itself, and naught can part thee from thy lord again. Go, then, to where she holds her court in a pleasant valley by the sea, and forget not that the gods bless tenfold those who waste not the power that is given them, how feeble soe'er it be."

So saying, she faded slowly away till Psyche found herself standing once more before the pale white statue. Then she turned and went through the silent temple, and out into the sunlight, and asked for the road which would lead her to the sea and Aphrodite's pleasant vale.

IX

For many a long day she journeyed, till at length she saw the blue sea far away and a pleasant valley sloping to the shore. Here the waves broke in laughing ripples on the beach, and the leaves danced gaily on the trees in the soft west wind; for Aphrodite, born of the foam, the fairest of all the goddesses, held her court there, surrounded by her nymphs and maidens. As she sat on her golden throne they danced around her with their white arms gleaming, and crowned her with roses, singing the while the song of her beauty.

"O foam-born Aphrodite, Queen of Love, fairest of Time's deathless daughters. Thee the golden-snooded Hours kiss as they pass and the circling Seasons crown with grace. Before thee all was fire and chaos, but at thy coming like sped to like. The earth decked herself with flowers, and the nightingale sang to her mate on the bough, and in the pale moonbeams youth and maiden sped hand in hand through the glade. Thy smile is like sunshine on ripples, but the flash of thine eyes like the death-bearing gleam of the lightning; for not always art thou kind. The heart of the scorner thou breakest, and art jealous for thy rites. Wherefore north and south and east and west men worship thee, both now and evermore, O goddess of ten thousand names!"

As Psyche drew near the nymphs espied her. With loud cries they rushed forward, and flinging chains of roses about her, dragged her forward before the throne.

"A prisoner, a prisoner!" they cried—"a mortal, O queen, who has dared to enter thy sacred vale! What fate shall be hers?"

And Psyche knelt trembling before the throne. She dared not look up, for she felt the eyes of the goddess upon her, and the blaze of her anger burned through to her heart.

"Psyche, what doest thou here? Knowest thou not that long ago I loved thee not, because thy beauty taught men to forget my dues, and mine own son didst thou lead to disobey my word? By thy folly hast thou lost him; and glad am I that he is rid of thy toils. Think not that thy tears will move me. Those who enter my sacred vale become the lowest of my slaves, and woe to them if they fail to do the task I set them. Verily, thine shall be no light one, or I am not the Queen of Love and Beauty."

"O lady," answered Psyche, "'twas to be thy slave and to do thy will that I came to thy sacred vale, if haply I might turn thy wrath to love and prove myself not all unworthy of thy son. Great was my sin, O goddess, when I doubted him; but many are the tears I have shed, and weary the way I have wandered in search of him — yea, even to the dark underworld would I go, if so be it I could find him there. As for the worship that men paid me, Zeus, who searcheth all hearts, knoweth that I lifted not mine in pride above thee. Nay, doth not every gift of beauty come from thee, O mighty one? If my face hath any fairness, 'tis that it shadoweth forth thine image. Weak are the hearts of men, lady, and hard is it for them to look on the sun in his might. Be not angry, then, if through the mortal image that perisheth, they stretch forth blind hands towards the beauty that fadeth not away. And now on my knees I beg thee, O queen, to set me thy hardest tasks, that I may prove my love or die for mine unworthiness."

As Psyche was speaking the face of the goddess softened, and she answered her more gently.

"Thy words please me, maiden, for the gods love those who shrink not back from trial. Three tasks will I set thee, and if in these thou fail not, one harder than all the others will I give thee, whereby thou shalt win thy love and immortality. Go, maidens, and lead her to my garner, that she may sort the golden grain ere the sun's first rays gild the pine-tops."

X

At the command of the goddess the nymphs gathered round Psyche, and, binding her hands with chains of roses, led her away to the garner. Here they set her free, and with peals of merry laughter bade her farewell.

"Pray to the hundred-handed one, maiden, to help thee," cried one; "thy two hands will not go far."

"Nay, an hundred hundred hands could not sort the grain by sunrise," said another.

"Better to work with two hands," said Psyche, "than idly to pray for ten thousand."

But for all her brave answer her heart sank as she looked at the task before her; for she stood in the largest garner it had ever been her lot to see— wide and lofty as her father's palace-halls, and all the floor was strewn with seeds and grain of every kind—wheat, oats and barley, millet, beans and maize, which she must sort each after its kind into a separate heap before the sun should rise. However, she set diligently to work, and minute after minute, hour after hour passed swiftly by, and the heaps kept growing by her side; yet for all her toil 'twas but a tiny corner of the garner she had cleared. Feverishly she worked on, not daring to look at what remained to do. Her back ached, her arms grew stiff, and her eyes felt heavy as lead, but she worked as one in a dream, and her head kept falling on her breast for weariness, till at length she could hold out no longer, but fell fast asleep upon the cold stone floor.

While she slept a marvellous thing happened. From every hole and crack there appeared an army of ants—black ants, white ants, red ants—swarming and tumbling over each other in their haste. Over the whole floor of the garner they spread, and each one carried a grain of seed, which it placed upon its own heap and ran quickly back for another. Such myriads were there, and so quickly did they work, that by the time the first ray of the sun peeped in at the windows the floor was clear, save for the heaps of sorted grain standing piled up in the midst. The bright light pouring in at the window fell upon Psyche as she slept, and with a start she awoke and began feverishly to feel about for the grain. When her eyes became accustomed to the light, how great was her joy and thankfulness to see the neat heaps before her! And as she looked round, wondering who could have been so kind a friend, she saw the last stragglers of the ants hurrying away to every crack and cranny.

"O kind little people," she cried, "how can I thank you?"

She had no time to say more, for the door was thrown open, and in a golden flood of sunlight the nymphs came dancing in. Seeing the floor cleared and the bright heaps lying on the floor, they stopped short in amazement.

"Verily thou hast wrought to some purpose, maiden," said one.

"Nay, she could never have done it of herself," said another.

"True, O bright-haired ones!" answered Psyche. "I toiled and toiled, and my labour did but mock me, and at length my strength gave way and I fell asleep upon the floor. But the little folk had pity on me, and came out in myriads and sorted out the grain till all was finished. And lo! the task is accomplished."

"We will see what our queen shall say to this," they answered.

And binding her once more in their rosy chains, they led her to Aphrodite.

"Hast thou swept my garner, Psyche, and sorted the grain each after its kind?" she asked.

"Thy garner is swept and thy grain is sorted, lady," she replied, "and therein I wrought the little

174

my feeble strength could bear. When I failed the little folk came forth and did the task."

Trembling, she waited for the answer, for she feared that in the very first trial she had failed. But Aphrodite answered,

"Why dost thou tremble, Psyche? The task is accomplished, and that is all I ask; for well do I know the little folk help only those who help themselves. Two more tasks must thou do before I put thee to the final proof. Seest thou yon shining river? On the other bank graze my flocks and herds. Precious are they beyond all telling, for their skins are of pure gold. Go, now, and fetch me one golden lock by sunset."

So saying, she signed to the nymphs to release Psyche, who went at once towards the stream, light-hearted; for this task, she thought, would be no hard one after the last.

As she approached the river she saw the cattle feeding on the further bank—sheep and oxen, cows and goats—their golden skins gleaming in the sunlight. Looking about for some means of crossing, she espied a small boat moored among the reeds. Entering it, she unloosed the rope and pushed out into the stream. As she did so, one of the bulls on the further shore looked up from his grazing and saw her. With a snort of rage he galloped down the field, followed by the rest of the herd. Right down to the water's edge they came, lashing their tails and goading with their horns, and an ill landing would it have been for Psyche had she reached the shore. Hastily she pushed back among the reeds, and pondered what she must do; but the more she thought the darker grew her lot. To get one single hair from the golden herd she must cross the stream, and, if she crossed, the wild bulls would goad her to death. At length in despair she determined to meet her doom, if only to show that her love was stronger than death. As she bent over the boat to loose the rope, a light breeze set the reeds a-whispering, and one seemed to speak to her.

"Fair lady, leave us not, for those who reach the further shore return not to us again."

"Farewell, then, for ever, gentle reed, for I have a task to do, though I die in the vain attempt."

"Ah, lady, stay here and play with us. Too young and fair art thou to die."

"No coward is young or fair, kind reed. And before sunset I must win a lock from a golden fleece yonder, or I shall never find my love again."

And she let loose the rope.

"Stay, stay, gentle maiden. There I can help thee, for all my life have I watched the golden herds, and I know their ways. All day long they feed in the pleasant pasture, and woe to those who would cross over when the sun is high in heaven. But towards evening, when he is sinking in the far west, the herdsman of Aphrodite cometh and driveth them home to their stalls for the night. Then mayest thou cross with safety and win a lock from the golden herd."

But Psyche laughed aloud at his words.

"Thou biddest me steal the apples when the tree is bare. Thy heart is kind, O reed, but thy tongue lacketh wisdom. Fare thee well."

"Not so fast, lady. Seest thou not the tall ram yonder by the thorn-bush? Sweet grows the grass beneath its shade, yet to reach it he must leave a golden tribute on the thorns. Even now there is a lock of his fleece caught in the branches. Stay with us till the herds are gone, lady, and then canst thou win the lock of gold."

"O kindest of reeds, forgive my blindness. 'Tis more than my life thou hast saved, for, with the task undone, I should lose my love for ever."

So all day long she stayed and talked with the reeds; and they told her that often folk came down to the stream and pushed out for the other bank. But when the cattle rushed raging to the water's edge they turned back afraid, and dared not venture forth again, but went home disconsolate. And so they heard not the whispering of the reeds nor learnt the secret of winning the golden lock.

Now the shadows were falling fast, and away in the distance Psyche heard the horn of the herdsman and his voice calling the cattle home. At the sound they lifted their heads, and made for the gate on the far side of the field. As soon as they were safely through, Psyche pushed out the boat and rowed to the other bank. Swiftly she made for the thorn-bush and picked the golden lock from the bough, and as the boat glided back to the reeds, the sun sank low behind the hills. Close at hand she heard the laughter of the nymphs as they came to see whether the task were done. With a smile she drew the lock of gold from her bosom, and, marvelling, they led her back to Aphrodite.

"Thou hast a brave heart, Psyche," said the goddess, as she looked at the golden lock at her feet.

"The bravest heart could not have won this lock, lady, without knowing the secret which the reeds whispered to me."

"Well do I know that, Psyche. But 'tis only the pure in heart that can understand the voice of the wind in the reeds; and thus doubly have I tried thee. Take now this crystal bowl for thy third task. Beyond this pleasant vale thou wilt come to a dark and barren plain. On the far side a mighty mountain rears his peak to heaven, and from the summit a spring gushes forth and falls headlong over the precipice down into the gulf below. Go now and get me a draught of that stream, but see that thou break not the goblet on the way, for its worth is beyond all telling."

In truth, as she held it out, the crystal gleamed brighter than the rainbow. Psyche took the goblet, and the first rays of the sun found her already on the plain. Far away on the other side the mountain-peak rose barren and black against the sky, and she hurried on as fast as her feet would go, lest night should fall ere she had filled the goblet. On and on she went, and at length she drew near to the mountain and looked about for a path leading up to the summit. But naught could she see save rocks and boulders and masses of crumbling stones, and there was nothing for it but to set to work to climb the rough mountain-side. Clasping the goblet tightly in one hand, she clung to the rocks as best she might with the other, fearing at every step that she would slip and break her precious burden. How she ever reached the top she never knew, but at length she stood, bruised and torn, upon the summit. What was her dismay when she saw that the mountain-peak was divided by a mighty cleft, and across the abyss she saw the stream of water gushing out from the steep rock a hundred feet and more below the summit! Even had she toiled down again and up on the other side the rock fell away so smooth and sheer that a mountain-goat would have no ledge on which to rest his foot.

Psyche sat down upon a rock to think what she must do, and the more she thought the more she felt that her last hour had come.

"For the only way I can reach the water is to throw myself into the bottomless abyss, where the stream flows deep down into the bowels of the earth; and I should be dashed to pieces, but perchance the King of the Underworld would have mercy on me, and let my soul return but once on earth to bear the crystal bowl to Aphrodite."

So saying, she stood and bade farewell to the earth and the pleasant sunlight and the fair flowers that she loved, and prepared to throw herself over the mountain-side. As she was about to spring from the edge, she heard the whirring of wings above her head, and a mighty eagle flew down and settled on the rock beside her.

"Far up above thy head, in the blue sky, have I watched thee, Psyche, and seen thy labours on the mountain-side. Too brave and true art thou to go to thy death. Give me the goblet, and I will fill it.

Knowest thou that yonder stream is a jet which springeth up from dark Cocytus, the River of Wailing, which watereth the shores of the dead? No mortal can touch of that water and live, or bear it away in a vessel of earth. But this goblet is the gift of Zeus almighty, and I am his messenger—the only bird of heaven that can look on the sun in his might. Give me the cup, then, and I will fill it, and bear it to the mountain-foot, that thou mayest carry it back in safety."

With tears of joy and thankfulness Psyche gave him the goblet, and as he flew away across the dark chasm, swift as an arrow from the bow, she turned and sped down the mountain-side, heeding not the stones and boulders, so glad was she at heart. At the foot she found the eagle awaiting her.

"O mightiest of birds, how can I thank thee?" she cried.

"To have served thee, lady, is all the thanks I need. Farewell, and may the gods prosper thee in thy last great trial."

And he spread his mighty wings and flew away. Psyche watched him till he grew but a tiny speck in the blue of the sky. Then she turned and hastened across the plain with her precious goblet of water.

The nymphs danced out to meet her as before, and led her to Aphrodite.

"I see thou art fearless and true, maiden," she said, when Psyche had told her tale. "Twice hast thou faced death without flinching, and now must thou go down to his own land; for no woman is worthy of my son's love, if she possess not beauty immortal that fadeth not with passing years. And she alone, the Queen of the Dead, can give thee this gift. Take this casket, then, and go and kneel before her and beg her to give thee therein the essence of that beauty. When thou hast it, see thou hasten swiftly back and open not the casket; for if its fumes escape and overcome thee in the world below, thou must dwell for ever with the shades."

So Psyche took the casket, and her heart sank within her at the thought of that dread journey. And the nymphs waved sadly to her as she went away, for never yet had they looked on one who had returned from the dark land of shadows.

XI

Away from the pleasant vale went Psyche, for she knew full well that nowhere in that fair place could she find a way down to the world below. As a child, when she had lived in her father's halls, her nurse had told her strange tales of dark and fearsome caves which men called the mouth of Hades, and how those who went down them never returned; or if one perchance, more favoured than the rest, came back into the sunlight, his face was pale and his strength departed, and he talked wildly of strange things that none could understand.

Far over the country-side she wandered and asked for the gate of Hades, and some pitied her weakness, and some laughed at her foolishness, and all men thought her mad.

"For beggar and king, for wise and foolish, the road to Hades is one," they said, "and all must travel it soon or late. If thou seekest it, in very sooth, go throw thyself from off yon lofty tower, and thou wilt find it fast enough."

Sadly she went and stood on the tower, for she saw no other way. Once again she bid farewell to the earth and the sunlight, and was about to leap from a pinnacle, when she thought she heard a voice calling her by name, and she hushed her breath and listened.

"Psyche, Psyche," she heard, "why wilt thou pollute my stones with blood? I have done thee no wrong, yet thou wouldst make men hate me and shun the rock on which I stand. As for thee, it would avail thee nought, for thy soul would dwell for ever in the Kingdom of the Dead, and the shadow of thyself, faint and formless, would glide about my walls, and with thin-voiced wailing weep for thy lost love; men, hearing it, would flee from me, and for lack of the builder's care, my stones would fall asunder, and of all my proud beauty naught would be left, save a mound of moss-grown stones and thy spirit's mournful guardianship."

Then Psyche knelt and kissed the stones.

"Poor tower," she said, "I would not harm thee. Thou canst tell me, perchance, some better way, for I must bear this casket to the Queen of the Dead, and beg for a gift of beauty immortal, that I may return to the earth worthy of my lord."

"Hadst thou thrown thyself over the edge, thou wouldst never have come to the Queen of the Dead, but wailing and forlorn wouldst have wandered on the shores of the Land that has no name; for betwixt that land and Hades flows the wide Stygian stream. One boat there is that can cross it, and therein sits Charon, the ferryman of souls. Greedy of gain is he and hard of heart, and none will he take across who bear not a coin of gold in their mouths. And the pale ghosts of those who have died away from their loved ones, when none were by to pay the last rites of the dead and place the gold coin in their mouths—all these flock wailing around him and beg him with heart-rending cries to take them over the stream. But to all their entreaties he turneth a deaf ear and beateth them back with his oar. E'en hadst thou prevailed on him and come to the palace of pale Persephone, thou couldst not have entered in; for at the gates sits Cerberus, the three-headed hound of Hell, and none may pass him without a cake of barley-bread. But his soul loveth the taste of earth-grown corn, and while he devours it the giver may pass by unscathed."

"The coin of gold and the barley-cake I can get," she said, "but how I can reach the Under-world alive I know not."

"Not far from hence thou wilt find the cave men call the Gate of Hades. In ignorance they name it, for no man hath proved where it leads. All the long years I have stood upon this rock have I watched the entrance to that cave, and men have come up and looked inside, and the boldest have entered in; but always have they come swiftly back, staggering like drunken men, with pale faces and wild eyes full of fear, and about them hangs the smell of the noisome vapours that rise up from the gates of the dead; and the old wives sitting by the fireside nod their grey heads together. ''Tis the tale that our mothers told us long ago and their mothers before them,' they mutter. ''Tis surely the

Gate of Hades, and those who venture too far will never come back again.' They have guessed aright, maiden, and down that dark cavern lies thy path."

"But if those who venture too far never return, how shall I bear back the essence of undying beauty in the casket?"

"Instead of one gold piece, take two, and two loaves of fresh-baked barley-bread. One gold coin to the ferryman and one loaf to the hound must thou give as thou goest, and keep the rest for thy return, and from greed they will let thee pass back again. Tie the casket in thy bosom, and put the gold coins in thy mouth, and take the barley-loaves one in each hand. See that thou set them not down, or the pale ghosts will snatch them away; for the taste of the earth-grown meal giveth a semblance of warmth to their cold forms, and for a brief space they feel once more the glow of life. So by many a wile will they seek to make thee set down the bread; but do thou answer them never a word, for he who toucheth or answereth one of these becometh even as they are."

Psyche thanked him for his counsel, and went forth to beg the two gold coins and barley-loaves, and for love of her fair face the people gave it gladly. When all was ready, she set out towards the cave. About its mouth the brambles grew tall and thick, and the ivy hung down in long festoons, for none had ventured in for many a long year. As best she might, she cut a way through the prickly hedge, and stood in the shadow of the cave, and the drip of the water from the roof sent a faint echo through the vaults. Through the dark pools she went, through mud and through mire, and the green slime hung like a dank pall about the walls. On and on she hastened, till her head swam round and her heart turned sick within her; for round her floated a mist of poisonous vapour, which choked her and made her gasp for breath, and monstrous shapes swept past—the Furies and Harpies and hundred-headed beasts which guard the gate to Hades. Their cries and shrieks filled the air, and every moment she shrank back, terrified that they would tear her limb from limb, as they bore down on her with the whirr of their mighty wings and their wild locks flying in the wind. Across the path they stood and waved her back, and her heart turned cold with fear; but she pressed onward with hurrying steps, and lo! when she came up to them the shapes clove asunder like mist before the sun, and she passed through them, and found they were but smoke.

And so she came to the nameless land that lies betwixt earth and Hades; a barren, boundless plain it is, with never a tree or shrub to break the dulness of its sad mud flats. Up and down it wanders the shades of those whose bodies the kind earth has never covered, and they wring their hands and wail to their dear ones above, to grant them burial and the rites of the dead. For Charon, the grim ferryman, beats them back from his boat, because they have no coin, and they are doomed to dwell for ever in the land that has no name.

As she was crossing the dismal plain, an old man came towards her beating a laden ass. Old and weak was he, and could scarce stagger along by the side of the beast, and as he came up to Psyche the cords broke that bound the burden on the ass's back, and the faggots he carried were scattered all about. And he set up a dismal wailing, and wrung his pale withered hands.

"Gracious damsel, have mercy on an old man, and help me load my ass once more."

But Psyche remembered the words of the tower, and she clung the tighter to the loaves of bread, though she longed to help the feeble shade.

Onward she went till she came to the banks of the Styx, the mighty river of Hell, by which the great gods swear. Nine times it winds its snaky coils about the shores of Hades, and across its leaden waters Charon, the boatman of the dead, ferries backward and forward for ever. When he saw Psyche, he hailed her, and asked her for the coin. Answering him never a word, she held out one coin with her lips, and as he took it she shuddered. For his breath was as the north wind blowing across the snow, and his eyes were like a fish's, cold and dull.

"Welcome, sweet maiden. 'Tis not often we get a fare like thee, my boat and I;" and he laughed a hard, thin laugh, like the cracking of ice in a thaw, and beneath her weight the boat creaked in chorus.

Out into the stream he pushed with his pole, and then set to with his oar, and the rise and fall of the blade made never a sound in those dull leaden waters. As they neared the middle of the stream, Psyche saw two pale arms rise up above the waves, and the head of an old man, who cried out to her piteously,

"Help, help! I drown in this foul stream! Ah, for pity's sake put out one finger to save me!"

And Psyche turned aside to hide her tears; for the face was the face of her father, and his cries pierced through to her heart. As the boat passed by he sank with a moan beneath the waves, and she saw him no more.

At length they reached the shore of Hades, and she saw three paths before her leading upwards from the landing-stage. As she stood, not knowing which to take, the old man beckoned to her.

"I know not whither thou art bound, lady, for thou bearest not on thee the mark of the dead. The souls of the wicked I know, for about them fly the Furies, the avengers of sin, and hound them down the left-hand path, through Periphlegethon, the river of fire—down, down to the utmost depths of Tartarus. And the souls of the brave shine forth like stars in the darkness, and they take the right-hand path to the Elysian fields of light, where the breeze blows bright and fresh and the golden flowers are glowing. The middle path leadeth to the palace of pale Persephone, but that way only the gods and the children of the gods may go, or those who bear with them some token from the Immortals."

Then Psyche showed him Aphrodite's casket, and turned up the middle path. Through a dark wood she went, and came out upon a plain. Here she saw three aged women weaving at a loom, and they cried out to her in weak, quavering voices,

"Oh, maiden, thine eyes are young and thy fingers supple. Come help us unravel the thread."

But for the third time she turned aside, and went quickly on her way, and when she looked back over her shoulder the loom and the hags had vanished away.

So at length she came to the palace of Persephone. The roof and columns were all of pure silver, which shone with a pale light through the murk and gloom, like the shimmer of pale moonbeams on a cloudy night. Above the heads of the pillars ran a frieze of strange device. It told of Night and Chaos, and of the birth of Time, and how the sons of Earth rose up against the gods in deadly battle, and were hurled into the depths of Tartarus by the thunderbolts of Zeus. And it showed how Prometheus the Titan gave fire to mortal men, so that they learnt all manner of crafts, and became the masters of all living things, and like the gods for wisdom. But they ruled by the law of the strongest, and said that might was right, and begat the foul forms of Pestilence and War and red-handed Murder. The other side told of the things that would come to pass when Time and Death should be no more, and Love should rule the universe. On that side all the forms were fair and all the faces beautiful, and the breeze played through pleasant places where the flowers never fade. In the centre of the pediment, with mighty wings overshadowing either side, stood a mighty figure, Anangke, great Necessity, the mother of gods and men. From the one side she looked dark and terrible, and the world trembled at her frown, but from the other she was fairer than the day, and by unchanging law she drew all things after her till they should be perfected.

On the palace steps before the doorway sat Cerberus, the three-headed watch-dog. When he saw Psyche approaching he began to growl, and his growl was like the rattle of thunder far away. As she drew nearer he barked furiously and snarled at her, baring his white gleaming fangs. Quickly she threw him one of the barley loaves, and while he was devouring it, she slipped gently past, and stood within the courtyard of the palace. All was silent and deserted, and her footsteps, as they fell on the marble pavement, sent no echo through the colonnades; for it seemed that even sound must die in that lifeless air. She passed through great doors of bronze into a lofty hall. In the shadowy depths of it she saw a great throne raised, and on it sat the Queen of the Dead. About her stood two handmaids, and their names were Memory and Sleep. One fanned her with great poppy-leaves, and as she did so the eyes of the queen grew heavy and dim, and she sat as one in a trance. But when this one grew weary of fanning, anon the other would hold up before her a great mirror of polished steel, and when she looked into it the colour would rush into her pale cheeks, and her eyes would glow like coals of fire, for in the flash of the steel she saw earth's flowery meadows, and remembered that for three months only did she live in the gloom and the shade; and she knew, moreover, that one day the circling seasons would stay their course, and decay and death would pass away, and when that time came she would return no more to the murk and gloom, but dwell for ever in the sunshine and the flowers. A magic mirror is that which Memory holds, and few are there who can bear to look on its brightness, but those whose eyes are strong gaze into its depths, and learn that knowledge and remembrance are one.

With timid steps did Psyche cross the hall, and knelt upon the steps of the throne.

"Child of Earth, what dost thou here?" asked the queen. "This is no place for living souls."

"O mighty one, 'tis a boon I beg of thee," said Psyche, and drew from her bosom Aphrodite's casket. "Give me, I pray thee, the gift of undying beauty in this casket, that I may return above worthy of my lord."

"'Tis a great boon thou askest. Nevertheless, for thy bravery's sake I will give it thee. For many are they who set out to find it, but few have the heart to come so far."

Thereupon she took the casket in her hands,

and breathed into it, and her breath was as the smoke of incense on the altar.

"Take it and return swiftly whence thou camest, and see thou open it not till thou comest upon earth. For in the land of the dead my breath is death, but above it is life and beauty immortal. Fare thee well."

With a glad heart Psyche rose from her knees, and sped through the silent palace. She threw the second loaf to Cerberus as she passed, and for the second coin of gold Charon took her once more across in his boat. This time no sad phantoms cried to her for help, and she knew that it was for the sake of the earth-grown meal that they had stood in her path before.

At last she stood once more in the sunlight, and joy lent wings to her feet as she sped across the plain and away to Aphrodite's pleasant vale. With the casket in her hand, she knelt before the throne, but Aphrodite put out her hand and raised her up.

"Kneel no more to me, Psyche, for now thou art one of us. But open the casket and drink into thy very soul the life and beauty that will never die."

Her smile was brighter than sunshine on the shimmering waves, and the touch of her hand made Psyche's blood run like fire through her veins. Scarce knowing what she did, she opened the casket. The fumes rose up in a cloud about her head, and she knew no more till she felt herself moving upwards, upwards. As life came slowly back she opened her eyes, and looked into the face of him she had seen but once. His rainbow wings were spread above her, and his strong arms held her close, and he looked into her eyes with the look that mingles two souls into one.

"Beloved," he whispered, "Love has conquered all things. In thy darkest hour of trial I watched over thee, and gave thee strength, and now we two will dwell for ever in the courts of heaven, and teach the hearts of men to love as we love."

Hyacinthus

"...The sad death
Of Hyacinthus, when the cruel breath
Of Zephyr slew him—Zephyr penitent
Who now, ere Phæbus mounts the firmament,
Fondles the flower amid the sobbing rain."
John Keats.

"Whom the gods love die young"—truly it would seem so, as we read the old tales of men and of women beloved of the gods. To those men who were deemed worthy of being companions of the gods, seemingly no good fortune came. Yet, after all, if even in a brief span of life they had tasted god-given happiness, was their fate one to be pitied? Rather let us keep our tears for those who, in a colourless grey world, have seen the dull days go past laden with trifling duties, unnecessary cares and ever-narrowing ideals, and have reached old age and the grave—no narrower than their lives—without ever having known a fulness of happiness, such as the Olympians knew, or ever having dared to reach upwards and to hold fellowship with the Immortals.

Hyacinthus was a Spartan youth, son of Clio, one of the Muses, and of the mortal with whom she had mated, and from mother, or father, or from the gods themselves, he had received the gift of beauty. It chanced one day that as Apollo drove his chariot on its all-conquering round, he saw the boy. Hyacinthus was as fair to look upon as the fairest of women, yet he was not only full of grace, but was muscular, and strong as a straight young pine on Mount Olympus that fears not the blind rage of the North Wind nor the angry tempests of the South.

When Apollo had spoken with him he found that the face of Hyacinthus did not belie the heart within him, and gladly the god felt that at last he had found the perfect companion, the ever courageous and joyous young mate, whose mood was always ready to meet his own. Did Apollo desire to hunt, with merry shout Hyacinthus called the hounds. Did the great god deign to fish, Hyacinthus was ready to fetch the nets and to throw himself, whole-souled, into the great affair of chasing and of landing the silvery fishes. When Apollo wished to climb the mountains, to heights so lonely that not even the moving of an eagle's wing broke the everlasting stillness, Hyacinthus—his strong limbs too perfect for the chisel of any sculptor worthily to reproduce—was ready and eager for the climb. And when, on the mountain top, Apollo gazed in silence over illimitable space, and watched the silver car of his sister Artemis rising slowly into the deep blue of the sky, silvering land and water as she passed, it was never Hyacinthus who was the first to speak—with words to break the spell of Nature's perfect beauty, shared in perfect companionship. There were times, too, when Apollo would play his lyre, and when naught but the music of his own making could fulfil his longing. And when those times came, Hyacinthus would lie at the feet of his friend—of the friend who was a god—and would listen, with eyes of rapturous joy, to the music that his master made. A very perfect friend was this friend of the sun-god.

Nor was it Apollo alone who desired the friendship of Hyacinthus. Zephyrus, god of the South Wind, had known him before Apollo crossed his path and had eagerly desired him for a friend. But who could stand against Apollo? Sulkily Zephyrus marked their ever-ripening friendship, and in his heart jealousy grew into hatred, and hatred whispered to him of revenge. Hyacinthus excelled at all sports, and when he played quoits it was sheer joy for Apollo, who loved all things beautiful, to watch him as he stood to throw the disc, his taut muscles making him look like Hermes, ready to spurn the cumbering earth from off his feet. Further even than the god, his friend, could Hyacinthus throw, and always his merry laugh when he succeeded made the god feel that nor man nor god could ever grow old. And so there came that day, fore-ordained by the Fates, when Apollo and Hyacinthus played a match together. Hyacinthus made a valiant throw, and Apollo took his place, and cast the discus high and far. Hyacinthus ran forward eager to measure the distance, shouting with excitement over a throw that had indeed been worthy of a god. Thus did Zephyrus gain his opportunity. Swiftly through the tree tops ran the murmuring South Wind, and smote the discus of Apollo with a cruel hand. Against the forehead of Hyacinthus it dashed, smiting the locks that lay upon it, crashing through skin and flesh and bone, felling him to the earth. Apollo ran towards him and raised him in his arms. But the head of Hyacinthus fell over on the god's shoulder, like the head of a lily whose stem is broken. The red blood gushed to the ground, an unquenchable stream, and darkness fell on the eyes of Hyacinthus, and, with the flow of his life's blood, his gallant young soul passed away.

"Would that I could die for thee, Hyacinthus!" cried the god, his god's heart near breaking. "I have robbed thee of thy youth. Thine is the suffering, mine the crime. I shall sing thee ever—oh perfect friend! And evermore shalt thou live as a flower that will speak to the hearts of men of spring, of everlasting youth—of life that lives forever."

As he spoke, there sprang from the blood-drops at his feet a cluster of flowers, blue as the sky in spring, yet hanging their heads as if in sorrow.

And still, when winter is ended, and the song of birds tell us of the promise of spring, if we go to the woods, we find traces of the vow of the sun-god. The trees are budding in buds of rosy hue, the willow branches are decked with silvery catkins powdered with gold. The larches, like slender dryads, wear a feathery garb of tender green, and under the trees of the woods the primroses look up, like fallen stars. Along the woodland path we go, treading on fragrant pine-needles and on the beech leaves of last year that have not yet lost their radiant amber. And, at a turn of the way, the sun-god suddenly shines through the great dark branches of the giants of the forest, and before us lies a patch of exquisite blue, as though a god had robbed the sky and torn from it a precious fragment that seems alive and moving, between the sun and the shadow.

And, as we look, the sun caresses it, and the South Wind gently moves the little bell-shaped flowers of the wild hyacinth as it softly sweeps across them. So does Hyacinthus live on; so do Apollo and Zephyrus still love and mourn their friend.

Artemis and Orion

There was another young hunter who encountered Artemis and her maidens in the woods, but he met with a kinder fate at the hands of the goddess than did poor Actæon, whose only fault had been a most natural curiosity.

The fleet-footed Artemis was no more ardent in the chase than was the hunter Orion, who roamed the forest all day with his faithful dog, Sirius. One morning, as he rushed eagerly through the woods in pursuit of a deer, he came suddenly upon the seven Pleiades,—nymphs of Artemis,—who were resting after a long and arduous hunt begun at daybreak. Charmed with their beauty, Orion drew nearer, but the maidens, terrified at his outstretched arms, fled away through the forest. Undaunted by the remembrance of Actæon's fate, the hunter pursued the flying nymphs, determined that so much beauty should not escape him. Seeing that he was gaining on them in spite of their swift feet, the maidens called upon Artemis for help, and were at once changed into seven white pigeons which flew up into the heavens before

Orion's astonished eyes. Sometime later these same Pleiades became seven bright stars, and were set as a constellation in the sky, where they have remained ever since.

Orion continued to hunt from early dawn until nightfall without any misfortune overtaking him on account of his impetuous love-making. On the contrary his ardor evidently found favor with the goddess Artemis, for one day, when he unexpectedly met her alone in the forest, she smiled graciously upon him and offered to share the day's sport with him. Perhaps it was the beauty of the young hunter as well as his boldness that charmed the goddess; but however that may be, she continued to meet him in the forest, and they hunted together hour after hour until the twilight began to fall. Then Artemis knew that she must leave her lover and mount her silver moon-car.

When Apollo learned of his sister's affection for the young hunter, he was very angry, for Artemis had refused the love of the gods, and had begged of Zeus the right to live unwed. The sun-god determined therefore to put an end to Orion's wooing. So he waited at the shadowy portals of the west until Artemis, her nightly journey over, descended from her silver car and threw the reins on the necks of her wearied steeds. Then Apollo spoke to his sister of her hunting, and praised her skill with the bow. Presently he pointed to a tiny speck that was rising and falling on the crest of the waves a long distance away, and bidding her use this as a target, he challenged her to prove her skill. Artemis, suspecting no treachery, fitted an arrow into her bow and let it fly with unerring aim. Great was her distress when she learned what her brother's trickery had led her to do; for it was no floating log or bit of seaweed that her arrow had pierced, but the body of Orion. Apollo had seen the hunter go each morning to the ocean to bathe, and he thought this an easy way to dispose of the unworthy lover.

Artemis mourned Orion many days; and to keep his memory honored she placed him and his faithful dog, Sirius, in the sky as constellations.

REWARDED BY THE GODS

For deities that were worshipped so dutifully across ancient Greece, it might be easy to conclude so far that the Greeks' devotion to their gods and goddesses was founded on fear. Make no mistake, however – the gods and goddesses of Greek myth could be as benevolent as they were cruel. The men and women of myth who won the favour of these mighty beings were rewarded liberally by their patrons. These three tales demonstrate the generosity of the gods and goddesses, whether out of genuine kindness or an ulterior motive. Paris is offered three very different incentives during a competition between Athena, Hera, and Aphrodite. Philemon and Baucis are rescued from a tragic fate by Zeus and Hermes thanks to their offer of hospitality. And finally, Idas and Marpessa's romantic union is blessed by the gods. Sometimes, after all, it all works out. For a while at least.

The Apple of Discord

There was once a war so great that the sound of it has come ringing down the centuries from singer to singer, and will never die.

The rivalries of men and gods brought about many calamities, but none so heavy as this; and it would never have come to pass, they say, if it had not been for jealousy among the immortals,—all because of a golden apple! But Destiny has nurtured ominous plants from little seeds; and this is how one evil grew great enough to overshadow heaven and earth.

The sea-nymph Thetis (whom Zeus himself had once desired for his wife) was given in marriage to a mortal, Peleus, and there was a great wedding-feast in heaven. Thither all the immortals were bidden, save one, Eris, the goddess of Discord, ever an unwelcome guest. But she came unbidden. While the wedding-guests sat at feast, she broke in upon their mirth, flung among them a golden apple, and departed with looks that boded ill. Some one picked up the strange missile and read its inscription: *For the Fairest*; and at once discussion arose among the goddesses. They were all eager to claim the prize, but only three persisted.

Aphrodite, the very goddess of beauty, said that it was hers by right; but Hera could not endure to own herself less fair than another, and even Athena coveted the palm of beauty as well as of wisdom, and would not give it up! Discord had indeed come to the wedding-feast. Not one of the gods dared to decide so dangerous a question,—not Zeus himself,—and the three rivals were forced to choose a judge among mortals.

Now there lived on Mount Ida, near the city of Troy, a certain young shepherd by the name of Paris. He was as comely as Ganymede himself,— that Trojan youth whom Zeus, in the shape of an eagle, seized and bore away to Olympus, to be a cup-bearer to the gods. Paris, too, was a Trojan of royal birth, but like Œdipus he had been left on the mountain in his infancy, because the Oracle had foretold that he would be the death of his kindred and the ruin of his country. Destiny saved and nurtured him to fulfil that prophecy. He grew up as a shepherd and tended his flocks on the mountain, but his beauty held the favor of all the wood-folk there and won the heart of the nymph Œnone.

To him, at last, the three goddesses entrusted

the judgment and the golden apple. Hera first stood before him in all her glory as Queen of gods and men, and attended by her favorite peacocks as gorgeous to see as royal fan-bearers.

"Use but the judgment of a prince, Paris," she said, "and I will give thee wealth and kingly power."

Such majesty and such promises would have moved the heart of any man; but the eager Paris had at least to hear the claims of the other rivals. Athena rose before him, a vision welcome as daylight, with her sea-gray eyes and golden hair beneath a golden helmet.

"Be wise in honoring me, Paris," she said, "and I will give thee wisdom that shall last forever, great glory among men, and renown in war."

Last of all, Aphrodite shone upon him, beautiful as none can ever hope to be. If she had come, unnamed, as any country maid, her loveliness would have dazzled him like sea-foam in the sun; but she was girt with her magical Cestus, a spell of beauty that no one can resist.

Without a bribe she might have conquered, and she smiled upon his dumb amazement, saying, "Paris, thou shalt yet have for wife the fairest woman in the world."

At these words, the happy shepherd fell on his knees and offered her the golden apple. He took no heed of the slighted goddesses, who vanished in a cloud that boded storm.

From that hour he sought only the counsel of Aphrodite, and only cared to find the highway to his new fortunes. From her he learned that he was the son of King Priam of Troy, and with her assistance he deserted the nymph Œnone, whom he had married, and went in search of his royal kindred.

For it chanced at that time that Priam proclaimed a contest of strength between his sons and certain other princes, and promised as prize the most splendid bull that could be found among the herds of Mount Ida. Thither came the herdsmen to choose, and when they led away the pride of Paris's heart, he followed to Troy, thinking that he would try his fortune and perhaps win back his own.

The games took place before Priam and Hecuba and all their children, including those noble princes Hector and Helenus, and the young Cassandra, their sister. This poor maiden had a sad story, in spite of her royalty; for, because she had once disdained Apollo, she was fated to foresee all things, and ever to have her prophecies disbelieved. On this fateful day, she alone was oppressed with strange forebodings.

But if he who was to be the ruin of his country

had returned, he had come victoriously. Paris won the contest. At the very moment of his honor, poor Cassandra saw him with her prophetic eyes; and seeing as well all the guilt and misery that he was to bring upon them, she broke into bitter lamentations, and would have warned her kindred against the evil to come. But the Trojans gave little heed; they were wont to look upon her visions as spells of madness. Paris had come back to them a glorious youth and a victor; and when he made known the secret of his birth, they cast the words of the Oracle to the winds, and received the shepherd as a long-lost prince.

Thus far all went happily. But Aphrodite, whose promise had not yet been fulfilled, bade Paris procure a ship and go in search of his destined bride. The prince said nothing of this quest, but urged his kindred to let him go; and giving out a rumor that he was to find his father's lost sister Hesione, he set sail for Greece, and finally landed at Sparta.

There he was kindly received by Menelaus, the king, and his wife, Fair Helen.

This queen had been reared as the daughter of Tyndarus and Queen Leda, but some say that she was the child of an enchanted swan, and there was indeed a strange spell about her. All the greatest heroes of Greece had wooed her before she left her

father's palace to be the wife of King Menelaus;*
and Tyndarus, fearing for her peace, had bound
her many suitors by an oath. According to this
pledge, they were to respect her choice, and to go
to the aid of her husband if ever she should be
stolen away from him. For in all Greece there was
nothing so beautiful as the beauty of Helen. She
was the fairest woman in the world.

Now thus did Aphrodite fulfil her promise and
the shepherd win his reward with dishonor. Paris
dwelt at the court of Menelaus for a long time,
treated with a royal courtesy which he ill repaid.
For at length while the king was absent on a journey to Crete, his guest won the heart of Fair Helen,
and persuaded her to forsake her husband and sail
away to Troy.

King Menelaus returned to find the nest empty
of the swan. Paris and the fairest woman in the
world were well across the sea.

* Menelaus actually became the king of Sparta through his marriage to Helen so it was her country they resided in.

Philemon and Baucis

Upon a hill in the land of Phrygia stands a thousand year old oak, and close by it a linden of the same age, both surrounded by a low wall. Many a wreath has been hung upon the boughs of the neighborly pair. Not far from them extends a swampy lake into which empties a shallow stream. Where in former times people dwelt, now only herons and ducks rove about. Once Father Zeus came to this spot with his son Hermes carrying only his wand, but not his winged cap. They were seeking hospitality in human form. They knocked at a thousand doors praying shelter for the night. But the people were so disobliging that the heavenly visitants could not anywhere find lodging. At the end of the village was a hut, humble and small, covered with straw and rushes. In this poor house lived a happy couple, honest Philemon and Baucis, his wife, of the same age. They had spent their joyous youth together there, and there they had grown white-haired. They made no complaint of their poverty, but quietly bore their hard lot, united in love, and although childless, they were content in the mean little house which they alone occupied together.

As the high deities approached this humble roof and entered the low passageway with bowed heads, the honest couple met them with a hearty greeting. The old man placed seats for them, and Baucis, clad in a coarse dress, begged them to rest themselves. The little mother busied herself about the hearth, stirred up the ashes, piled up dry leaves and brushwood, and kindled a fire. Then she brought split wood and placed it under the little kettle hanging over the fire. In the meantime Philemon brought cabbage from his well-watered garden, deftly unleaved it, took down a side of smoked pork with his two-tined fork from the ceiling, and cut a huge piece from the shoulder to put into the boiling water. That the time might not seem too long to the strangers, they exerted themselves to entertain them with light conversation. They also poured water into the wooden tub so that they could enjoy a foot bath. Smiling in a friendly way, the gods accepted these proffers, and while they were stretching their feet comfortably in the water their gracious host prepared the couch-bed, which stood in the middle of the room. The cushions were stuffed with rushes and the feet and frame were made of woven willow. Philemon brought carpetings which were only kept for feast days,—how old and poor they were!—and the divine guests prepared to enjoy the meal which was now ready. The little mother, in her neat apron, placed with trembling hands the three-legged table before the couch, and as it would not stand very securely, she raised it slightly by placing something under it. Then she rubbed the plates with fresh mint and food was set before them. There were olives, cornelian cherries, preserved in clear thick sirup, also radishes, endives, fine cheese, and eggs cooked in the ashes. Baucis brought all these in earthen dishes, besides a showily colored pitcher and neat cups of beechwood, glazed on the inside with yellow wax, filled with milk, for they had no wine. Nuts, figs, and dates were brought for dessert, and two dishes filled with plums and spicy apples. In the middle of the table was a whitish honeycomb. But the finest seasoning of the meal was the good friendly faces of the honest old couple, testifying to their honesty and generosity.

As all were enjoying the food and drink, Philemon observed that the pitcher contained wine instead of milk and that in spite of emptying of the cups they were continually refilled. Then he recognized with surprise and fear whom he was entertaining. In distress he flew to his old companion with upraised arms and downcast eyes and implored her to know what they should offer to their heavenly guests. Suddenly it occurred to them that they might offer their only goose. Both ran out, but the goose was faster than they. Hissing and flapping its wings, it ran here and there, outdistancing the old people. Finally it ran into the house and crouched behind the guests, as if seeking divine protection. And it did not seek in vain.

The guests restrained the ardor of the old people and said with a laugh: "We are gods who have come to earth to test the generosity of men. We found your neighbors wicked and they shall be punished. But you shall leave this house and follow us to the summit of the mountain, so that you shall not suffer with the guilty ones." Both obeyed, and leaning upon their staffs they wearisomely climbed the mountain. They were not an arrow's flight from the highest peak when they anxiously looked down and saw the whole place changed into a raging waste of waters, and of all the houses only their own little one remained. While they stood astonished and bewailed the fate of the others, behold the poor old hut towered above the waters as a temple. A golden roof was supported on its columns and its floors were of marble. Zeus turned to the trembling old people and said: "Tell me, honest old man and worthy wife of the honest old man, what do you most wish?" Philemon exchanged a few words with his wife and then said: "We would be your priests. Permit us to serve in that temple. And as we have so long lived together, let us die at the same hour. Then I shall never see the grave of my dear wife nor will she have to bury me."

Their wish was granted. As long as they lived they served in the temple. And once, when weary with the weight of age and years, they were standing on the sacred steps, thinking of their wonderful fate, Baucis saw her Philemon and Philemon his Baucis disappearing and floating away to the distant height. "Farewell, dear one. Farewell, beloved one," said each as long as they could speak. Thus ended the worthy pair. He was turned into an oak and she into a linden, and thus they remained as close together in death as they had been in life. Goodness is prized by the gods. They bestow honors upon those who prove themselves worthy.

Idas and Marpessa

By day, while the sun-god drove his chariot in the high heavens and turned the blue-green Ægean Sea into the semblance of a blazing shield of brass, Idas and Marpessa sat together in the trees' soft shades, or walked in shadowy valleys where violets and wild parsley grew, and where Apollo rarely deigned to come. At eventide, when, in royal splendour of purple and crimson and gold, Apollo sought his rest in the western sky, Idas and Marpessa wandered by the seashore watching the little wavelets softly kissing the pebbles on the beach, or climbed to the mountain side from whence they could see the first glimpse of Artemis's silver crescent and the twinkling lights of the Pleiades breaking through the blue canopy of the sky. While Apollo sought in heaven and on earth the best means to gratify his imperial whims, Idas, for whom all joys had come to mean but one, sought ever to be by the side of Marpessa. Shadowy valley, murmuring sea, lonely mountain side, or garden where grew the purple amaranth and where roses of pink and amber-yellow and deepest crimson dropped their radiant petals on the snowy marble paths, all were the same to Idas—Paradise for him, were Marpessa by his side; without her, dreary desert.

More beautiful than any flower that grew in the garden was Marpessa. No music that Apollo's lute could make was as sweet in the ears of Idas as her dear voice. Its music was ever new to him—a melody to make his heart more quickly throb. New, too, ever was her beauty. For him it was always the first time that they met, always the same fresh ravishment to look in her eyes. And when to Idas came the knowledge that Marpessa gave him love for love, he had indeed won happiness so great as to draw upon him the envy of the gods.

"The course of true love never did run smooth," and, like many and many another father since his day, Evenos, the father of Marpessa, was bitterly opposed to a match where the bridegroom was rich only in youth, in health, and in love. His beautiful daughter naturally seemed to him worthy of something much more high. Thus it was an unhappy day for Marpessa when, as she sat alone by the fountain which dripped slowly down on the marble basin, and dreamed of her lover, Idas, Apollo himself, led by caprice, noiselessly walked through the rose bushes, whose warm petals dropped at his feet as he passed, and beheld a maiden more fair than the fairest flower that grew. The hum of bees, the drip, drip of the fountain, these lulled her mind and heart and soothed her day-dreams, and Marpessa's red lips, curved like the bow of Eros, smiled as she thought of Idas, the man she loved. Silently Apollo watched her. This queen of all the roses was not fit to be the bride of mortal man—Marpessa must be his.

To Evenos Apollo quickly imparted his desire. He was not used to having his imperial wishes denied, nor was Evenos anxious to do so. Here, indeed, was a match for his daughter. No insignificant mortal, but the radiant sun-god himself! And to Marpessa he told what Apollo wished, and Marpessa shyly looked at her reflection in the pool of the fountain, and wondered if she were indeed beautiful enough to win the love of a god.

"Am I in truth so wondrous fair?" she asked her father.

"Fair enough to mate with Apollo himself!" proudly answered Evenos.

And joyously Marpessa replied, "Ah, then am I happy indeed! I would be beautiful for my Idas' sake!"

An angry man was her father. There was to be no more pleasant dallying with Idas in the shadowy wood or by the seashore. In the rose garden Apollo took his place and charmed Marpessa's ears with his music, while her eyes could not but be charmed by his beauty. The god had no doubts or fears. Only a little time he would give her, for a very little only would he wait, and then undoubtedly this mortal maiden would be his, her heart conquered as assuredly as the rays from his chariot conquered the roses, whose warm crimson petals they strewed at his feet. Yet as Marpessa looked and listened, her thoughts were often far away and always her heart was with Idas. When Apollo played most exquisitely to her it seemed that he put her love for Idas into music. When he spoke to her of his love she thought, "Thus, and thus did Idas speak," and a sudden memory of the human lad's halting words brought to her heart a little gush of tenderness, and made her eyes sparkle so that Apollo gladly thought, "Soon she will be mine."

And all this while Idas schemed and plotted and planned a way in which he could save his dear one from her obdurate father, and from the passion of a god. He went to Poseidon, told his tale, and begged him to lend him a winged chariot in which he could fly away with Marpessa. Poseidon good-naturedly consented, and when Idas flew up from the seashore one day, like a great bird that the tempests have blown inland, Marpessa joyously sprang up beside her lover, and swiftly they took flight for a land where in peace they might live and love together. No sooner did Evenos realise that his daughter was gone, than, in furious anger against her and her lover, he gave chase. One has watched a hawk in pursuit of a pigeon or a bird of the moors and seen it, a little dark speck at first, gradually growing larger and more large until at length it dominated and conquered its prey, swooping down from above, like an arrow from a bow, to bring with it sudden death.

So at first it seemed that Evenos must conquer Idas and Marpessa in the winged chariot of Poseidon's lending. But onwards Idas drove the chariot, ever faster and faster, until before the eyes of Marpessa the trees of the forest grew into blurs of blue and brown, and the streams and rivers as they flew past them were streaks of silver. Not until he had reached the river Lycormas did the angry father own that his pursuit had been in vain. Over the swift-flowing stream flew the chariot driven by Idas, but Evenos knew that his horses, flecked with white foam, pumping each breath from hearts that were strained to breaking-point, no longer could go on with the chase. The passage of that deep stream would destroy them. The fierce water would sweep the wearied beasts down in its impelling current, and he with them. A shamed man would he be forever. Not for a moment did he hesitate, but drew his sharp sword from his belt and plunged it into the breast of one steed and then of the other who had been so willing and who yet had failed him in the end. And then, as they, still in their traces, neighed shrilly aloud, and then fell over and died where they lay, Evenos, with a great cry, leaped into the river. Over his head closed the eddies of the peat-brown water. Once only did he throw up his arms to ask the gods for mercy; then did his body drift down with the stream, and his soul hastened downwards to the Shades. And from that day the river Lycormas no more was known by that name, but was called the river *Evenos* forever.

Onwards, triumphantly, drove Idas, but soon he knew that a greater than Evenos had entered in the chase, and that the jealous sun-god's chariot was in pursuit of the winged car of Poseidon. Quickly it gained on him—soon it would have swept down on him—a hawk indeed, this time, striking surely its helpless prey—but even as Apollo saw the white face of Marpessa and knew that he was the victor, a mighty thunderbolt that made the mountains shake, and rolled its echoes through the lonely fastnesses of a thousand hills, was sent to earth by

Zeus. While the echoes still re-echoed, there came from Olympus the voice of Zeus himself.

"*Let her decide!*" he said.

Apollo, like a white flame blown backward by the wind, withheld his hands that would have seized from Idas the woman who was his heart's desire.

And then he spoke, and while his burning gaze was fixed upon her, and his face, in beautiful fury, was more perfect than any exquisite picture of her dreams, his voice was as the voice of the sea as it calls to the shore in the moonlit hours, as the bird that sings in the darkness of a tropic night to its longing mate.

"Marpessa!" he cried, "Marpessa! wilt thou not come to me? No woe nor trouble, never any pain can touch me. Yet woe indeed was mine when first I saw thy fairest face. For even now dost thou hasten to sorrow, to darkness, to the dark-shadowed tomb. Thou art but mortal! thy beauty is short-lived. Thy love for mortal man shall quickly fade and die. Come to me, Marpessa, and my kisses on your lips shall make thee immortal! Together we shall bring the sunbeams to a cold, dark land! Together shall we coax the spring flowers from the still, dead earth! Together we shall bring to men the golden harvest, and deck the trees of autumn in our liveries of red and gold. I love thee, Marpessa—not as mere mortal loves do I love thee. Come to me, Marpessa—my Love—my Desire!"

When his voice was silent, it seemed as if the very earth itself with all its thousand echoes still breathed his words: "Marpessa—my Love—my Desire."

Abashed before the god's entreaties stood Idas. And the heart of Marpessa was torn as she heard the burning words of the beautiful Apollo still ringing through her head, and saw her mortal lover, silent, white-lipped, gazing first at the god and then into her own pale face. At length he spoke:

"After such argument what can I plead?
Or what pale promise make? Yet since it is
In woman to pity rather than to aspire,
A little I will speak. I love thee then
Not only for thy body packed with sweet
Of all this world, that cup of brimming June,
That jar of violet wine set in the air,
That palest rose sweet in the night of life;
Nor for that stirring bosom all besieged
By drowsing lovers, or thy perilous hair;
Nor for that face that might indeed provoke
Invasion of old cities; no, nor all
Thy freshness stealing on me like strange sleep.

Nor for this only do I love thee, but
Because Infinity upon thee broods;
And thou art full of whispers and of shadows.
Thou meanest what the sea has striven to say
So long, and yearned up the cliffs to tell;
Thou art what all the winds have uttered not,
What the still night suggesteth to the heart.
Thy voice is like to music heard ere birth,
Some spirit lute touched on a spirit sea;
Thy face remembered is from other worlds,
It has been died for, though I know not when,
It has been sung of, though I know not where.
It has the strangeness of the luring West,
And of sad sea-horizons; beside thee
I am aware of other times and lands,
Of birth far-back, of lives in many stars.
O beauty lone and like a candle clear
In this dark country of the world! Thou art
My woe, my early light, my music dying."

—STEPHEN PHILLIPS.

Then Idas, in the humility that comes from
perfect love, drooped low his head, and was silent.
In silence for a minute stood the three—a god, a
man, and a woman. And from on high the watching stars looked down and marvelled, and Artemis
stayed for a moment the course of her silver car to

watch, as she thought, the triumph of her own invincible brother.

From man to god passed the eyes of Marpessa, and back from god to man. And the stars forgot to twinkle, and Artemis's silver-maned horses pawed the blue floor of the sky, impatient at the firm hand of the mistress on the reins that checked their eager course.

Marpessa spoke at last, in low words that seemed to come "remembered from other worlds."

For all the joys he offered her she thanked Apollo. What grander fate for mortal woman than to rule the sunbeams—to bring bliss to the earth and to the sons of men? What more could mortal woman crave than the gift of immortality shared with one whose power ruled the vast universe, and who still had stooped to lay the red roses of his passionate love at her little, human feet? And yet—and yet—in that sorrow-free existence that he promised, might there not still be something awanting to one who had once known tears?

"Yet I, being human, human sorrow miss."

Then were he indeed to give her the gift of immortal life, what value were life to one whose beauty had withered as the leaves in autumn, whose heart was tired and dead? What uglier fate than this, to endure an endless existence in which no life was, yoked to one whose youth was immortal, whose beauty was everlasting?

Then did she turn to Idas, who stood as one who awaits the judgment of the judge in whose hands lies the power of meting out life or death. Thus she spoke:

> "But if I live with Idas, then we two
> On the low earth shall prosper hand in hand
> In odours of the open field, and live
> In peaceful noises of the farm, and watch
> The pastoral fields burned by the setting sun.
> And he shall give me passionate children, not
> Some radiant god that will despise me quite,
> But clambering limbs and little hearts that err.
> . . . So shall we live,
> And though the first sweet sting of love be past,
> The sweet that almost venom is; though youth,
> With tender and extravagant delight,
> The first and secret kiss by twilight hedge,
> The insane farewell repeated o'er and o'er,
> Pass off; there shall succeed a faithful peace;
> Beautiful friendship tried by sun and wind,
> Durable from the daily dust of life."

The sun-god frowned as her words fell from her lips. Even now, as she looked at him, he held out his arms. Surely she only played with this poor mortal youth. To him she must come, this rose who could own no lesser god than the sun-god himself.

But Marpessa spoke on:

"And thou beautiful god, in that far time,
When in thy setting sweet thou gazest down
On his grey head, wilt thou remember then
That once I pleased thee, that I once was young?"

So did her voice cease, and on the earth fell sudden darkness. For to Apollo had come the shame of love rejected, and there were those who said that to the earth that night there came no sunset, only the sullen darkness that told of the flight of an angry god. Yet, later, the silver moonbeams of Artemis seemed to greet the dark earth with a smile, and, in the winged car of Poseidon, Idas and Marpessa sped on, greater than the gods, in a perfect harmony of human love that feared nor time, nor pain, nor Death himself.

Glossary

Acteon	hunter punished by Artemis
Adonis	mortal loved by Aphrodite
Amphitrite	goddess of the sea
Apollo	god of music and healing
Arachne	weaver who became a spider
Ares	god of war
Artemis	goddess of the hunt
Athene/Athena	goddess of wisdom and war
Baucis	mortal woman and wife of Philemon
Cronos	titan and god of time
Deucalion	son of the titan Prometheus
Demeter	goddess of the harvest
Dionysus	god of wine
Eos	personification of dawn
Eris	goddess of discord
Eros	god of love
Epimetheus	titan and brother of Prometheus
Gaea	goddess of earth
Hades	god of the underworld
Hebe	goddess of youth
Helen	the most beautiful woman on earth

Hera	goddess of marriage
Heracles	hero and half mortal son of Zeus
Hermes	the messenger god
Hephaestus	god of craftsmanship
Hesperus	personification of the evening star
Hestia	goddess of the hearth
Hyacinthus	mortal lover of Apollo
Leto	titan and goddess of motherhood
Idas	mortal man and lover of Marpessa
Io	mortal woman transformed into a heifer by the gods
Marpessa	mortal woman and lover of Idas
Menelaus	king of Sparta and husband of Helen
Nereids	minor sea deities
Niobe	queen of Thebes
Nymphs	minor nature deities
Oceanus	titan and early god of the sea
Olympian	third and final generation of Gods, ruled by Zeus
Olympus	the mountain on which the gods and goddesses resided
Orion	mortal lover or friend of Artemis
Rhea	titan and goddess of fertility
Pandora	the first mortal human
Paris	prince of Troy
Pentheus	king of Thebes

Persephone	goddess of spring and queen of the underworld
Philemon	mortal man and husband of Baucis
Poseidon	god of the sea
Prometheus	titan and brother of Epimetheus
Psyche	wife of Eros
Pyrrha	daughter of Epimetheus and Pandora
Tartarus	the deepest part of the Underworld
Titans	the second generation of gods, ruled by Cronos
Typhoeus	monstrous son of Gaea
Uranus	god of the sky
Zephyrus	personification of the west wind
Zeus	god of lightning and king of Olympus

MACMILLAN COLLECTOR'S LIBRARY

Own the world's great works of literature in one beautiful collectible library

Designed and curated to appeal to book lovers everywhere, Macmillan Collector's Library editions are small enough to travel with you and striking enough to take pride of place on your bookshelf. These much-loved literary classics also make the perfect gift.

Beautifully produced with gilt edges, a ribbon marker, bespoke illustrated cover and real cloth binding, every Macmillan Collector's Library hardback adheres to the same high production values.

Discover something new or cherish your favourite stories with this elegant collection.

Macmillan Collector's Library: own, collect, and treasure

Discover the full range at
macmillancollectorslibrary.com